Year

Of

Sanctuary

By

Kaz Peacock

[1]

Realisation is a strange and often painful sensation. Not unlike the moment you swallow something too hot and you know that once it is past your throat, there is no stopping that uncomfortable, ricocheting journey until it hits your gut. That's when decisions need to be made.

It was the photograph that started it. I had come across it during one of my many culling sessions, which I often throw myself into in order to avoid taking control of any bigger issues.

The photograph; taken of my 18 year old self, after the loss or I should say the death of both my parents, because after all I would never find them again. I do vaguely remember a well meaning aunty taking me out to a spiritual retreat in Turkey which she was sure would help my emotional health. That photograph showed a depth of sadness in my eyes and an unnatural emptiness which I did not know how to handle. My world had imploded, then subsequently exploded, sending me spiralling into the unknown.

I wish I had studied that picture sooner.

None the less, it had succeeded in triggering the realisation moment. Now here I was 27 years later; sat in my doctor's surgery, waiting for the final punch to reach its destination.

***

'So, you are experiencing panic attacks?'

Dr. Simpson spoke without averting his eyes from his computer screen.

'Am I?' I responded, immediately on the defensive.

'Well that *is* what your symptoms would suggest.'

Tap tappity-tap on his keyboard. The positioning of the monitor was set at an angle, which didn't quite allow me to see what intimate information he was sharing, almost like a schoolboy hiding his work. He could be playing hangman for all I knew.

Leaning forward slightly I attempted an intent stare, willing him to make eye contact.

'Erm—I don't think I mentioned the word panic.'

'You feel vulnerable in certain situations?'

I wondered if this was a question or an accusation.

'Well I suppose I...'

'You mentioned difficulty with breathing and cold sweats?' he eyed my glistening upper lip; well at least I had his attention.

'I...I guess so.' I muttered whilst trying to dab away the moisture with an already damp tissue. My throat was feeling parched and I began nervously scanning the room for access to drinking water. He barely disguised his look of smugness as he swivelled back towards the keyboard. It was at that moment that my flight or fight response kicked in and within a matter of seconds my body decided on the flight option. I half rose from the chair but I instantly felt giddy and nauseous, so as my legs began to lose their solidity I managed a graceful descent back to my seat. The medicine man appeared not to have noticed my plight as he continued.

'Right, I have prescribed you a course of mild anti-depressants which should help. I will also refer you to a medical counsellor. I would like to see you again in one month's time and we will see how we get on shall we?'

He ripped off the prescription print-out with a final flourish and I snorted indignantly at this last comment which suggested that he would be joining me for my happy pill ride.

With a raise of his eyebrows he turned to face me and joined his hands in a prayer like gesture. Uh-oh.

'Mrs Rowland, with all due respect, things are bound to feel difficult for you...you are at an age now when maybe you should be considering...'

Oh, my god, what was he going to suggest, suicide? A retirement home, euthanasia perhaps?

I'm only forty-five years old! So before he could say HRT I was up and out of his room striding purposefully along the corridor, desperately looking for the light at the end of the tunnel.

'Bollocks, crap...' I groaned as I did a sudden about turn and sloped meekly back to his office. I tapped gently on the door and walked over to his desk where he appeared to have frozen in prayer. I reached over and picked up the prescription.

'Sorry, forgot this,' and then as an afterthought, 'Oh and you might want to check my details. I am *Miss Peters* now...I have been for sometime.' I smiled weakly, 'I'll let you know how I get on.'

As I reach the doorway I glance over to see that he was indeed intently checking my details, well either that or he was now playing patience.

***

'It's as if I wake up and forget who I am you know? I mean it's not a memory thing; it's more a placement thing. I feel I know who I am but I don't know where I should be going. It's as if I no longer have a purpose and I have lost my direction. I mean I can be in a room full of people and feel invisible. I feel I am constantly battling against the flow; it's like wading through treacle. Do you understand?' Great sobs and splutters were being projected towards this poor person who until that day I had never had the reason or the courage to meet. He looked scared, possibly because he was paid to listen *to* but not participate *in* this gruelling performance. He handed me a box of tissues with an almost convincing sympathetic smile, 'Mrs Rowland; Dr. Simpson feels that attending these sessions will help you to cope with your panic attacks, so we may need to do some deep soul searching. I do realise this can be quite stressful. May I ask how old you are?'

I licked my lips like salted wounds and straightened my self with a shuddering sigh,

'My name is *Miss* Cassie *Peters,* I am forty-five years old and I think I am going to be just fine.'

I felt I knew this to be true because the only person who could truly help me was myself. I was the benefactor of all my personal baggage so it was up to me to rid myself of the excess; and besides, I seemed to be the only person who could get my sodding name right.

[2]

I was sitting at my kitchen table eyeing the bottle of pills when Jenny knocked on my back door and entered as usual, uninvited. 'Good Lord,' she spluttered, 'what on earth are you doing?' She dramatically grabbed the bottle of pills, knocking over a carton of milk in the process. I stood up and calmly reached past her for some kitchen roll, while she continued to cling suspiciously to the tablets, 'Erm, well actually Jen,' I said casting her a sideways grin. 'I was just wondering what to do with those little pink bombers... after all if I'm not going to make any use of them, I wouldn't want them falling into the wrong hands...if you know what I mean?'

With a little shock of recognition Jenny quickly replaced the small brown bottle on the table and pushed it towards me as if it was about to explode.

'I do apologise Cassandra, I thought...you know...'

'Well actually, no...I don't know Jen; you'll have to enlighten me.'

I threw the soggy kitchen roll into the bin and crossed to the sink to wash my hands making a mental note not to allow the sourness to take hold. I pulled up a chair to face her. 'Surely, you can't think I am that weak?'

She was staring at the table; people did seem to have trouble looking me in the eye these days.

'No-no, it's just that...well, you have been a bit low recently and not quite yourself.'

'How do you mean?'

'Well, sort of vacant.'

'As opposed to being engaged?' Jenny didn't get my joke.

'No-I mean as if you're not with us any more.'

I thought she sounded quite sad when she said this, but I understood, invisible, I thought. Jenny looked a little uncomfortable and puzzled by her own revelation so we stayed silent for what seemed a long while. It was very unlike Jenny to be silent.

4

Jenny's was what I called an imposing friendship, in that she wasn't really a true friend but more someone who thought I needed her companionship; a do-gooder who didn't always do a tremendous amount of good; a know-all who knew very little apart from everybody else's business. She had attached herself to me and for some unknown reason I felt obliged to allow her into my life. I don't even remember how we first met, a friend of a friend of a colleague at some uneventful work do probably. I did know that she *didn't* work, she had no need to because 'she and Brian were very comfortable thank you very much...' whatever the fuck that meant. I had never been to her home, had never been invited and never felt the need to visit. Jenny spent all of her free time, (and I am quite certain of this) cruising the streets of the social housing developments that straggled the outskirts of our Surrey town; in her top of the range racing green Mercedes, searching for those less fortunate than herself. Although, I'm not so sure everyone would concur with that opinion. Jenny had no children and no family in the near vicinity so I guess that is why I and a few other chosen ones felt we should help to fill her life. It kept her busy until Brian returned home from whichever office he was ensconced in all day. I didn't dislike Jenny exactly but she had the uncanny knack of making me feel angry and sorry for her at the same time.

I got up to put the kettle on for the inevitable cup of tea and I took the opportunity to break the all-enveloping silence.

'Jenny, how do you feel?' I kind of knew as soon as the words escaped my lips that this wasn't going to be an easy conversation.

'I beg your pardon?' she was picking through the biscuit tin—possibly searching for something chocolate covered amongst the anaemic Rich Teas, I dared to hope that she was searching for an appropriate answer to my question.

'Well, do you feel any shifting in your life?' I poured the tea along with my heart.

Her face suddenly gained that self-righteous, self-important look that I knew only too well. I had let my guard down damn it. Too late.

'Well, of course dear, I suffer from hot flushes as badly as the rest of us I'm sure.' She lowered her voice and looked around as if she was making sure nobody else was invading our conversational space, 'Brian moves into the spare room when I'm not feeling…well you know…he is so good like that bless him.' She ended the sentence with a funny downturn of her mouth, almost a grimace of disgust. I had absolutely no idea what the fuck she was talking about, but I'm sure Brian knew when he was on to a good thing.

'No—no, not physical changes,' I remonstrated, 'I mean the feeling that you need to be somewhere else, <u>anywhere</u> else….even someone else.'

Jenny nodded slowly giving the false impression that for one moment she understood my anguish. The moment was all too brief.

'Oh, Lord no, Brian would hate that, he wouldn't want me to be anyone else. He is always saying that I never cease to amaze him!'

I was beginning to have a certain amount of empathy with Brian.

'I don't think you are quite getting this Jen.'

'Well, who would dear, I mean you are rather different.'

I bit the bait. 'Different to who exactly Jenny?' I felt the heat rising in my chest, which was in danger of becoming volcanic as I trembled inwardly.

'Well, to all of us really.' This was said so matter of factly. Then as she reached for another biscuit I slammed the lid of the tin shut which made her flinch just for a second but then she cupped her hands around her now empty mug before resuming her attack. Oh, she was enjoying this.

Leaning back in her chair she continued, 'I mean let's face it Cassandra we are all suffering with this menopausal thingy, but none of us have changed to the extent that you have; but then we *do* have the support of our partners.'

Her bright red lips were pursed up in enjoyment of the words that were coming from her smart little mouth, sent by her dumb little brain. Still I said nothing which gave her licence to continue.

'It must be very difficult for you dear, being alone.'

6

She had that, 'you know it makes sense' look on her face.

'Jenny, you're not making any sense. What about Lucy, she's alone too.'

Mistake. I knew what was coming next and I could have ripped out my tongue for deserting me.

'Ah, yes but that was different dear, he died rest his soul, he didn't leave her for someone else.'

She wriggled into a more defiant position as though she had just emerged triumphant from battle.

I exhaled heavily and submitted my palms to the ceiling,

'Shit, so that's it then, that's the answer?' I slapped my hand to my forehead and watched her nodding sympathetically, 'Of course! All I need is a man to make my life complete, someone to stop me from becoming invisible, a good man to guide me down life's rocky path,' I continued dreamily, 'Maybe... ooh maybe.. I should give your Brian a ring!'

Bull's eye! Jenny glared at me and looking a little flushed and flustered she carefully placed her mug gently on the table, then she rose slowly, picked up her Gucci scarf and handbag and tucked her chair in with great precision.

'You know Cassandra; you really ought to seek some professional help.'

I was already standing with the door open ready for her to leave.

'Thanks Jenny.' I forced a warm smile that seemed to offend her even more, and then gently closed the door behind her.

I was so tired. My smile faded and the tears came once again.

[3]

It was a Sunday evening and I was feeling a little worse for wear, so I was hoping that I had just sent a text message to my son. When the caller ID confirmed he was returning my call I was still not entirely convinced.

'Ben?' I asked tentatively, just in case I was about to vent my emotions on some unsuspecting individual.

'Ma?' I suspected that *his* uncertainty was due to the fact that I had half a box of Kleenex stuffed up my nose... minus the cardboard of course.

'Ben,' I sniffled, 'Ben-ja-min.' I gulped.

'Ma...are you ok?' the concern was now evident in his voice.

I took a deep breath and continued shakily, 'Ben...as your mother...I would like your honest opinion, and I don't want you to hold back you understand...I can take the truth,' I paused, 'Do you think, I look like a man?' My voice was just at that strained point where it was teetering on the verge of total collapse and I was struggling to maintain control.

'Ma , what are you on about,' he giggled nervously, 'more to the point what are you *on*?'

Time to come clean.

'Well, just a tiny bit of weed from Dodgy Dave,' I said this while attempting to demonstrate the miniscule amount using my forefinger and thumb, 'but I think maybe I should *not* have had the two triple vodkas; or was it three double vodkas? Oh, anyway Ben it was so very stupid of me.' This admission came with a shuddering sigh.

'Mother! You don't even drink vodka!' he exclaimed.

'I know right?!' I readily agreed as if it was a revelation. There followed a short silence.

'Blimey, Dodgy Dave, is he still around? He must be getting on a bit!' Ben laughed.

'Yes, aren't we all?' I sobbed.

'Ma, what's wrong?' he asked gently, 'You haven't had the photo albums out again have you?'

'No of course not,' I quickly shuffled the albums under the cushions guiltily. 'I'm just feeling a bit low Ben; I'm so sorry pet I shouldn't have called you.'

Then I was crying again painfully aware of how awful this must be for him. He let out a weary sigh. 'Ma, I have heard this so many times. You need to stop all this before you make yourself ill. Ma, are you still there?'

'Where else would I be?' I responded self-pityingly but I instantly regretted it as I sensed a lecture coming on.

'Look, it's been six years now. You have to put an end to this morbid obsession with the past and move on. Imagine what it would have been like, for all of us, if you and Dad had stayed together. It really is time to let it all go Ma...start a new chapter, after all I have.'

This last statement slapped me with a sting. 'Christ, Ben I am truly sorry. I am such an awful mother,' I sniffed, 'and I've got no sodding Kleenex left!' a slight infusion of humour as I realised how pathetic I must seem.

'Well, I've got a few bog rolls here if you're desperate. Listen, why don't you come and stay for a few days?'

He said it like he really meant it.

'Oh Ben, do you really mean that?' I asked hopefully.

'I wouldn't ask otherwise, but don't make me regret it. Oh and by the way, never berate yourself as a mother; take it from one who knows. You may be a complete nutter but you just have to look at this fine specimen to see what a great job you do!'

I couldn't argue with that and by the end of our conversation I instantly felt lighter, I just hoped that Ben wasn't feeling the transferral of that weight. Having agreed I would visit the following weekend, I had something good to focus on and was eager to make that feeling last, so I immediately started to plan my journey to Cardiff.

[4]

Ben shared a student house. I often wondered if this indicated that it was a building in the process of becoming fully qualified whilst accommodating its inhabitants. Anyway, Ben shared the house with three other male students, all of who were quite used to me. It had occurred to me that the other three boys didn't seem to have such frequent visits from their parents as poor Ben did from me; this concerned me, as it possibly indicated that I was unfashionably needy. The four boys were in their second year of each other's company and still seemed to be getting along well considering how diverse their characters were.

Graham, was from Leeds and was studying theatre and media, he described himself as 'an adjustable gay.' When I asked what he meant by that, he explained, 'Well, mam and dad seem to think I will grow out of it and that I just need time to adjust to university life. I know they will get there in the end, they are lovely parents Cassie, just very traditional, and I need to be patient with them.'

I then rather clumsily enquired if he was comfortable sharing a house with three straight guys.

He looked vaguely amused 'Fuck yeah...they're me mates yer know!'

At the other end of the spectrum was alpha male Joseph who had been born in a leafy London suburb and being from healthy, wealthy stock could probably afford to have a luxury flat in Cardiff Bay. Both of Joe's parents were lawyers in the city and fully expected him to follow in their footsteps, this was a little disconcerting given his crash and burn mentality. Joe was handsome and charming but he had very little respect for his string of girlfriends and very little time for anything that didn't involve recreational pleasure. Joe called me 'honey' and would tap me on the backside when he passed by. I was concerned for him but was grateful that he actually wasn't mine to worry about.

Then there was Matthew from Southern Ireland, he was studying Economics and Business studies and hoped to make big things of his parent's farm back home. Mattie was a gentle, softly spoken lad who clearly adored his family and who probably suffered more from homesickness than he was prepared to let on; being the most organised member of the household, he would often spend time preparing spreadsheets to ensure that all the bills were divided equally and that every body took it in turn to keep the place looking semi-respectable. Not surprisingly, he had a long-term girlfriend, Alice, who had already been given the seal of approval from mammy and the rest of the folks back home. Matt and Ben were probably the closest in character and so they had become good friends, often going in search of the local pubs where they could sit and talk quietly about anything and everything till closing time. I felt and hoped that their friendship would be one that lasted well past their student years.

That left Ben, the listener and peacemaker. My son had an emotional trait, which he probably inherited from me, and a rarely seen flash of temper usually provoked by injustice. He was studying English Literature and Social History, with no idea where it would lead him, 'It'll come to me ma.' He was so laid back that it sometimes worried me, which was only natural I guess but at the same time I was sure I had been like that once and secretly wanted him to hang on to his 'no problem' attitude.

So this eclectic mix made for a reasonably harmonious household and I often speculated as to what would happen to each of them when they finally went their separate ways.

I arrived at Cardiff Central on a very wet Friday afternoon in February, 'horizontal rain' the Welsh called it and it was sharp enough to cut right through you. I wasn't relishing the prospect of trying to hail a cab outside the station, so when I saw Ben's familiar figure in the distance my heart gave a little tug. They do say that your child's walk and stance are almost as individual as a thumbprint and that the characteristic stays with them well into their adult years; I wonder if that's how other animals make out their offspring in a herd? Ben leaned into the weather but still managed to wear a welcoming grin as well as an expensive looking leather jacket and I wondered briefly if that had come out of his student loan but forgot to ask.

'Hello love,' I squeaked as I received a trademark Ben bear hug, 'I hope you're not missing a lecture.'

'Yeah, of course Ma, I have cancelled all of them for the next two weeks in honour of your visit!'

'I'm not staying for two weeks!' I laughed.

'Thank fuck for that. Just testing. Actually, I have every Friday afternoon free so my weekend starts here!' then he clicked his fingers together in that infuriating 'street' style that I had never been able to master without incurring some injury.

Ben leaned across to take my bag from beside me, and then feigning difficulty he stumbled and winced, 'Christ mother, just how long *are* you staying?'

'Oh, I'm so sorry Ben; you could have done without me spoiling your weekend.'

'Nonsense ma, you know you are always welcome, especially when my washing basket's full.'

We both smiled at this old joke and fell into a brief silence.

'Right, are you ready to make a break for it?'

'Sure, why not?'

Ben took the lead shouting and running through puddles like a child while I followed trying to dodge the back splash he was leaving in his wake, by the time we reached the old rust bucket he affectionately called his Ferrari, I was in fits of laughter and absolutely drenched.

'Oy, how come I am in a worse state than you are? I spluttered.

He looked up from putting my bag in the boot, 'Because, dear mother, *I* know how to look after myself.' Ouch.

Gallantly he struggled to open the passenger door, which I noticed had no working lock. Raising my eyebrows I deposited myself on the litter strewn front seat. Ben shot me an apologetic grin and then asked, 'Are you ok ma?' I knew he wasn't referring to my immediate comfort.

'Of course I am silly—just a little blip. You know me; I'll soon get over it. Besides I'm feeling loads better already!' I leaned over to pat his stubbly cheek and he didn't flinch.

'Good,' he sighed with relief, 'well I hope you brought some glad rags—because we're taking you out tonight!'

He turned the ignition and while the car juddered into life, I raised my voice to be heard, 'Erm, who?'

Driving off he paused for concentration, 'Oh, just me and the lads, don't panic, it's only down to the Union Bar for an open mike night, jeans and a tee-shirt will do. We thought you might enjoy a journey into the wild side of Uni life!'

We stopped at some traffic lights and I half turned to him, 'Ben, you haven't discussed this with everyone have you?'

The gears scrunched harshly, which I was sure was a deliberate avoidance tactic.

'Ben?'

'Erm...of course not. Well, just Mattie, Graham and Joe. Oh and Alice.'

I groaned and slid down into the now soggy seat.

'What?' he asked incredulously, 'Well, I had to clear it with them first—you know, the visitors rule—but they were all totally cool with it and besides they know what you're like by now and they love it when you come to stay.'

'Oh *great*, that makes me feel *so* much better.' I snorted, but I couldn't resist a little wry smile.

[5]

Forty-five years old is probably not the ideal age to spend a Friday night in a Student Union bar. There may have been a scattering of *older* students secreted in the darkened corners, although I was unsure when the word mature ceased to embody those beyond thirty years old. I wouldn't go so far as to say it was a bad experience but it served as a very strong reminder to me, that no matter how much I yearned for my youth, it was an era best not revisited. I felt an uncomfortable flash from the past in the form of a young girl vomiting with audible vigour over the back of one of the vinyl-covered sofas. Unfortunately, the young lady in question was not best dressed for the occasion and as her knees sunk further into the gaping mouth of the ripped foam filled furniture she was displaying a little more flesh than I am sure she intended. A small, but overly enthusiastic audience had gathered, and in their jeering midst was Joe, drunkenly drawing smiley faces on her exposed rear with a felt tipped pen—as if the poor girl would need reminding of the incident.

'Cheer up darling, the sun shines out of your arse!' he guffawed loudly. The little shit.

I was just beginning to feel very uncomfortable with the situation and I was wondering how best to intervene when Ben stepped in; much to the disappointment of Joe and his cohorts, he calmly told them enough was enough and directed them back to the bar, he then enlisted two other students to rescue the victim from her plight and all three tottered and swayed towards the exit.

I wasn't sure if Ben had come to the rescue for my benefit but I liked to think he would have done it anyway. He came to sit by me and placed my replenished pint of Guinness in front of me. 'First years,' he tutted, 'they'll soon learn. Sorry ma, this was supposed to be a bit more chilled but a lot of the bands dropped out and some of these kids are just getting over coming back from Christmas with their families.' He grimaced apologetically.

'Do you think it indicates that they miss home or they are just celebrating their freedom?' I enquired. This opened up a discussion by those hunched around our sticky little table about the memories of their first year away from home. Some were amusing, others were downright disgusting and a few were pretty scary if they were to be believed. I thanked god for that parental proviso, out of sight out of mind.

Once empty glasses were jostling for space on the table we decided to head back to the house collecting a small party of people as we left. As soon as we got in I retreated to the kitchen to make myself a cup of strong tea; then avoiding the patches of penicillin growth, I cleared and cleaned an area on the work surface. I had stopped off to buy some bread and local cheeses in Cardiff earlier so I was pretty confident I could produce some reasonably edible cheese toasties. As I busied myself with the task in hand I kept thinking back to the incident in the bar and felt the relief of being past that age but I just couldn't put my finger on where that left me now. I felt that all things considered, I had been a fairly successful adolescent, but I had never quite made it through to the next stage, like some un-evolved pupa. So, what was so wrong with that? It isn't written that life has to be rushed, that is how opportunities are missed; besides some people just take a little longer to realise what it is they truly want.

I was jolted from my reverie when I realised the Jenga stack of toasties had reached toppling level. I searched around for a suitable receptacle and found a deep baking tray to lay the sandwiches in, then grabbing a jumbo roll of kitchen towel I went forth to distribute sustenance to the masses. I was greeted with enthusiastic applause and beery kisses. I found Ben deep in conversation with a petite brunette who was being passionately animated about Amnesty International, I was reluctant to interrupt but he spotted me from the corner of his eye.

'Hey ma! This is Kate—Kate this is my lovely, long suffering ma.' He slurred.

'Hi Bens' Ma, nice to meet you.' Kate stepped forward to give me a hug, she had a gentle open smile and I wanted her to stay there wrapped in conversation with my son without any further interruptions from me.

'Its lovely to meet you too Kate but I hope you will forgive me if I don't stop to chat; I'm a bit out of practice with the 'all nighters' and I am pretty knackered!' Turning to Ben I asked, 'Just remind me where I'm sleeping tonight son and I'll be making my way to bed.'

I sensed Ben's relief but had to admire his ability to remain considerate.

'I moved your bag to the smallest room at the back of the house,' then as if reading my mind, 'and no I don't mean the toilet! In fact, it isn't even close to the bathroom, so you shouldn't be disturbed, there is even a lock on the door to keep out any strays!' he glanced at Kate with a smile to show how well he was looking after me.

'Thanks love, I realise that two a.m. is early by your standards but right now I think I will sleep through anything.'

Then without any hesitation or embarrassment he gave me a big hug. 'I'm glad you're here Ma, I hope you enjoyed yourself tonight.'

'It's been... an education.' I reached into the pocket of my jeans and pulled out a small plastic pouch and handed it discreetly to Ben, 'Oh and Dodgy Dave sends his regards.'

'All right Ma!' he chortled.

Then suddenly feeling like some sleazy drug pusher I added, 'But go easy ok? Remember....'

'Everything in moderation.' He finished my sentence with a knowing nod of his head and a lazy smile.

Within half an hour I had said my good nights and by three o'clock I was cocooned in my sleeping bag, drifting off with the hazy buzz of music and lively conversation fading into the distance.

***

When I surfaced the next morning I tiptoed my way to the bathroom. I had a speedy shower, not least because of the bone chilling water but also because it was still relatively early and I didn't want to disturb anyone. Creeping back to the room my bare feet protested against tacky, grubby floorboards on the landing and I was already dreaming of taking a nice deep, hot bubble bath when I got home. I dressed quickly and made my way downstairs thinking perhaps I could warm up with a cup of coffee. I was pleasantly surprised to find Ben washing up in the kitchen. His hair was damp and he had on a clean sweatshirt so I guessed he must have beaten me to the shower.

'Hello darling, I didn't expect to see you up just yet.'

'Morning Ma, yeah, erm Kate had to leave early because she wanted to drive to see her folks, so I thought I would make her some coffee and eggs for the journey.' he smiled sheepishly.

'Awh, that was nice of you pet. I liked Kate, she seemed really sweet.' I resisted the urge to pry.

'Yeah, she is pretty cool.' was his guarded response.

Watch this space I thought to myself. I quickly changed the subject to save his increasing blushes.

'So, I thought perhaps I could treat you to brunch in town before I catch my train home; unless of course you have other plans?'

'That sounds lush Ma, but you know you can stay as long as you want don't you? I mean I don't want you going back feeling miserable.'

I pushed against his arm gently. 'Bless you, but as much as I would love to cramp your style even further, I have a lot of thinking to do. This was an excellent idea and it has been good for me, I always feel better after some Ben time...thanks love, and besides...I miss my bed!'

***

It was still raining steadily as we sheltered in Cardiff station to say our goodbyes but I felt somehow rested and lighter in my heart.

'Now make sure you don't let your studies slip. There will come a time when you have to allow just a little seriousness into your life and a degree may just come in handy,' I grinned, 'but otherwise; don't change for anyone.'

'Whoa, the oracle has spoken!' he threw his hands up in mock defeat.

We had one last hug before I reluctantly broke away and started to walk towards the barriers.

'Text me when you're home, yeah?'

'Will do and I'll give you a call next week.'

Once through the barriers I turned to wave and felt that familiar tug deep in my chest and the tightening in my throat that most parents experience when being separated from their children; but this time seemed a bit different, this time when Ben smiled back I realised that he was managing perfectly well without me. Ben, my one and only true success in life. It took me by surprise for a moment and I felt a little disorientated, as if time had stood still but everything around me was shifting; and for some reason I sensed that my life was about to change.

[6]

'No—I'm not certain that I had issues with my parents exactly; apart form the fact that they named me Hope.'

'Why did that worry you exactly erm... Cassie?'

'Well, a bit of a recipe for disaster don't you think?'

Oh Lord, I could see by his face that he wasn't quite on my wavelength, and why should he be.

'Look...Rob? Maybe I should explain, I came to my parents late in their lives so I can quite understand the reason they would find the name appropriate. It was only because I loved and respected them dearly that I didn't even consider swapping my first and middle names around until after they had both passed away. Then when my divorce became final it seemed the natural thing to do; whilst I was reverting to my maiden name I changed the order of my Christian names; ...new beginnings and all that. But just imagine the endless opportunities for kids with a cruel sense of humour to get their kicks. I suppose it got a little more upsetting once I had started High School; such a vulnerable time don't you think?'

I was transported back to the playground, standing alone with no social skills wondering why I felt so misplaced. I had been a child who carried a generous layer of 'puppy-fat' and as I was a brunette I was painfully aware of the soft, dark hair that covered my arms and upper lip. My mother would be forever consoling me, telling me that I had beautiful eyes and that 'the men abroad' considered my appearance a thing of beauty, comparing my hirsute embarrassment to the skin of a peach; this did very little for the image I had of myself. I thought I would have to travel some miles before being accepted. I desperately wanted to be regarded as some mysterious, artistic type. Frida Kahlo was my heroine, but instead I felt like a blubbery little seal pup trapped in the culling season.

'Please, continue' encouraged Rob warming to the subject, I hadn't even realised I had been speaking my thoughts aloud.

'So, I tolerated the usual prodding and name calling while I patiently waited for my adolescent physique to sort itself out.

19

The ugly duckling didn't quite emerge as a swan but at least I started being accepted after a fashion. If the boys couldn't decide on who to date they would quip, 'I mustn't give up Hope!' and once I was deemed as acceptable girlfriend material it was, 'There is always Hope.' One jackass dumped me declaring, 'I have lost all Hope'

I shook my head and sighed heavily.

Rob barely managed to contain his amusement. Possibly not the support I was hoping for; but then he said gently, 'Cassie, I think you have come a lot further than you give yourself credit for.'

Clutching those words, I left my final session of counselling. At the very least I had learned that I could not blame my parents for blessing me with a name, which in essence represented something pretty special to them at the time; nor, as my son so often pointed out to me, could I blame his father six years after our divorce. No, it was clear to me that my present state of mind was entirely my own fault. There was nothing to stop me from moving on; no ties, job, home, they were all things I could just walk away from without too much collateral damage. My few remaining friends and family would not find distance an issue. Someone once said, 'You have nothing to fear but fear it's self.'

Well, there was no time like the present. I was ready to take on the challenge and it actually felt quite liberating.

When I shared my decision with Lucy she surprised me by being almost as excited as I was.

'Cass—this is great! At long last you will start to live your dream!' her eyes were sparkling, 'when do you want to start looking—I mean you know I'm happy to come along?'

I blushed and shot her a grateful smile.

'Thank crap; I am *so* relieved; I was kind of selfishly relying on your support Luce. Commuting by train to Brighton might prove to be a very expensive and time consuming method of flat hunting...plus I would really value your input...of course I will provide the petrol money and we may have to try out various local establishments to get a feel for the area and...and...'

'Put the spade down before that hole gets any bigger,' she chuckled, 'you know I want to do this for you; I wouldn't miss it for the world. You are my dearest friend Cass, I love you and you deserve this, it's been a long time coming. It's so exciting!'

'Oy,' I prodded her playfully, 'you seem a bit too keen to see the back of me!'

'Now, you know that's not true—besides, I need a holiday home.'

***

The first time Lucy and I had met was when I had nervously arrived at a parent and toddler group with Ben, he was a little shy and I was keen for him to develop the social skills which I had seriously lacked in my youth, before he entered the education system. However, when I stood on the thresh hold of the local church hall, I was painfully aware which one of us lacked the confidence. The room seemed to be full of young women who were the models of motherhood and who apparently could look immaculate at the same time. I was sure I was the only one who had the remnants of toddler breakfast stuck in my hair or the tell tale damp patch on my lap which was emitting a slight soiled nappy odour. Just as I was plotting our escape by perhaps feigning that I had forgotten the changing bag (which was stupid as it was in danger of overbalancing the now empty buggy), I was pounced on by one of the leaders of the happy throng.

'Helloo, helloo, come in, come in, welcome, welcome!' I wondered if this woman had some unfortunate medical condition which resulted in repetitive speech. 'I'm Cindy with a C!' she beamed proudly at me with a sparkling white smile. Ping! The advert for toothpaste with the little diamond sparkle of light suddenly sprang to mind. Her beautifully manicured hand was shaking mine vigorously as she continued, 'So, who have we here?'

I assumed that she was referring to Ben who by this time was blissfully unaware of my trauma and happily playing already on the toy car mat, but she continued to hold my gaze. I am sure my mouth was open and I vaguely remember Cindy with a C barely pausing for breath whilst she explained how St. Josephs mother and toddler group was as much a space for mummy as it was for the children and that 'we all pitch in' to tidy at the end of each session. Tea and coffee could be found at the serving hatch where you could help yourself and leave the money in the cup—the empty one of course—haha—toilets could be found at the end of the hall through the door to the left, fire exits were here and here—(Cindy with the phonetically incorrect name *had* to be a frustrated air stewardess) buggies must be left at the door, this she delivered with a cursory glance at my over ladened perambulator—but you will know for next time and the charge of £2.50 is payable on arrival. No sooner were those words out of her mouth than her palm shot out accompanied by another 'ping' smile. I fumbled in my pocket and thankfully found some loose change that wasn't too sticky or fluff covered and handed it over. The hand snapped shut with such ferocity that I was sure she must have impaled her palm with her lurid pink talons. I worried that her next sharp intake of breath heralded another tirade of instructional speech but instead she leaned towards me like some monstrous Queen of Hearts and breathed, 'Marvellous, now mingle dear, mingle!' Then she was gone, clip-clopping authoritatively across the hall.

I found the nearest chair that was close to Ben and sank gratefully into it. 'Jesus, Ben you'd better be enjoying this.' I muttered under my breath.

'I am guessing a strong coffee wouldn't go amiss?'

I turned to the voice and there was Lucy, rescuing me for the first but by no means the last time. Lucy had two boys, William and Stephen. William was only a baby when we met and Stephen was a year older than Ben. Through the following years our boys became good friends only to drift apart after attending different middle schools but Lucy and I remained in constant contact and though we sometimes went for weeks at a time without meeting each other our friendship never faltered and stood the ultimate test of no questions asked when support was needed. Lucy would listen to my indignant wailing about Colin and his many conquests and she supported me throughout the whole separation phase and beyond.

Likewise, when Lucies' husband, Malcolm was diagnosed with cancer, there was no question that I would be there to help her through that difficult time. So, we had been friends for the best part of twenty years—always knowing that we would be there for each other but never being entirely dependant on one another. We had shared some really good times along with the tough ones and many, many bottles of wine. Walking became a great way to meet up, keep fit and catch up all at the same time and Brighton soon became a favourite haunt. It seemed the natural place to start my search for a new home.

[7]

On our third flat hunting visit, I was feeling a little despondent, we were stood in the Estate Agents and Lucy was gently remonstrating with me.

'Cass, look I think you may have to expand your horizons a teeny bit and lower your expectations. I mean, it isn't absolutely necessary for you to have a sea view *or* a second bedroom *and* the luxury of a balcony—we have looked at all these properties before and the price isn't going to change, except in the wrong direction. It may be time to compromise.'

'I know Lucy, and I am so sorry, you must be really fed up with all this—but it's just—the dream you know?' I said a little too petulantly whilst leafing through the folders on the table.

'Oh, Cassie, I just don't want you to be disappointed that's all. Maybe, you should settle for less to begin with and see how it goes?'

'Maybe you're right.' I nodded slowly.

'Erm, excuse me—Miss Peters?' the young estate agent interrupted, 'there may be a property of interest to you that has just come through this morning if you would like to take a look. It's *really* reasonable; in fact I have just finished re-checking the rent with the landlord, which is why I am a bit late displaying it. It really is quite special so I wouldn't waste too much time if I were you.'

I had no reason to doubt young Nigel, especially as we had been such frequent visitors over the past weeks he must have been getting as desperate as I was; still I felt a little dubious when he handed me the information, hot off the press. Lucy and I pored over the specifications with increasing disbelief. A spacious second floor flat, full of character, two bedrooms, newly renovated kitchen and bathroom, shared courtyard garden to the rear and small balcony with sea views to the front of the property. Highly recommended, a must see. As we scanned down the page and eventually came to the monthly rent, we slowly turned to each other and could barely suppress our grins.

'Oh my god Lucy—I can just about afford this one and it sounds perfect!'

'Well, we had better get round there and check it out then.' Lucy suggested.

As we stood on the doorstep admiring the Celtic designed door knocker my eyes were drawn to the name plaque above the Flat Numbers, SANCTUARY HOUSE;

'Oh the irony' grinned Lucy, I rolled my eyes but felt a little shiver of delight.

I secured the tenancy that very day by paying four months rent plus the deposit upfront, just in case Nigel discovered there had in fact been an error. Not once did I feel any doubts. From the moment I stepped over the thresh-hold onto the Terrazzo floor in the entrance hall; it all felt so incredibly right that it didn't even faze me to discover that the landlord preferred not to be involved and was happy to trust Nigel with his choice of tenant. It was the second time I'd had that odd life shift feeling, as if I was being guided in my decisions and at that time I was more than happy to be led in the direction of SANCTUARY HOUSE.

[8]

The familiar three long and two short raps on the door announced Jenny's arrival.

'Halloo!' she yelled as she let herself in uninvited. I hadn't seen her since the incident with the tablets; she stopped short on the threshold to my kitchen.

'What on *earth* are you doing?' she squeaked.

'Now—where have I heard that before Jenny?' I smiled gently without looking up from the task in hand.

'Well I'm sure I don't know dear....but what <u>are</u> you doing exactly?' she persisted.

She was hopping about from one foot to the other, her eyes darting around taking in the scene, like some curious little bird; a real Jenny wren.

'I'm packing.' I answered flatly.

'I can *see* that Cassandra, but this is not a weekend in Wales pack is it?' there was a hint of impatience in her tone as she scanned the various boxes.

'Nope.' I replied whilst concentrating on detaching myself from a large strip of parcel tape.

'Neither is it a walking holiday in Cornwall with dear Lucy is it?' She was showing signs of agitation now and though I was partly enjoying her discomfort, seeing her fretting was not as much fun as I had imagined. I sighed and looked at her with slight amusement.

'Why don't you phone a friend?'

A quiet stillness ensued in which I could hear the steady drip of the kitchen tap that would no longer be my problem.

'I thought *you* were my friend.' She almost whispered.

I had never seen the vulnerable Jenny and I felt the urge to hug her, but instead I reached over and softly brushed her arm.

'Bless you Jen—I think perhaps I am more one of your lost causes than a true friend, but you are right this is not a holiday pack.'

I continued to cover some pictures in bubble wrap, resisting the urge to start popping the little capsules of air, I have never understood why that gives so much satisfaction; maybe it's the sense of giving something its freedom.

Jenny remained silent. I was waiting for her to ask where I was going but then I realised that she probably didn't really care that much, because having lost me she couldn't reel me back in. I had almost forgotten she was in the room when she gave a small apologetic cough, 'Well, I hope you know what you are letting yourself in for.'

'Fuck, no,' I chortled, 'but I imagine I am going to have some fun finding out!'

Jenny's hand shot to her lips as though she had uttered the expletive herself.

'Look Jen, I'm sorry if I have been a disappointment to you. It's a habit of mine apparently,' I shrugged apologetically, 'but you must know, that *my* time is now.' This was a last attempt to find a glimmer of empathy but instead she sniffed in disdain and took a last look around my kitchen; she had always declined the invites to venture further beyond and into the sitting room. Then as she quietly moved towards the back door, her sense of defeat was evident but she could not resist a parting shot,

'Well, be certain to call me when you need my help.'

Then with a flounce she was gone.

I had imagined that packing away twenty-two years of my life would be considerably harder. I wondered where it had all gone but then remembered that I had disposed of a lot of painful memorabilia when my husband had left. There were boxes still sealed up and in storage after six years that I knew I could no longer ignore, so it was with some trepidation that I began opening them but I was determined to lighten myself of any emotional burden hidden therein. As I sifted through I realised that a lot of the items had been kept thinking Colin may see the error of his wandering ways and come home to us. Gifts from me seemed to feature highly on his dispensable list. In one unmarked box I discovered jumpers and shirts that still carried the faint scent of the cologne I used to buy for him; along with several books on football and golf purchased in the hope that he might spend some time at home reading them. At the very bottom of this box was a maroon cashmere scarf, as I picked it out it unravelled and something dropped from its soft folds. The item had obviously been carefully secreted there for a reason; a slight lump rose in my throat when I instantly recognised the small box that contained a pair of gold cufflinks. They had been a special Christmas present, a last ditch attempt to show him I cared. Colin knew how much I hated high street jewellery stores, they were so totally alien to me and I remembered my increasing horror as I looked at the ever-escalating price tags. I could not believe that I was about to part with my hard earned cash on an item that I found so cold and ugly, I would much rather have gone to Camden market and bought something bright, handcrafted and fun. The sales assistant had been smarmy and persistent. The cufflinks had to be classy and unique but not too overstated; in keeping with the majority of Colin's possessions. This was a man who couldn't go for wet day walks for fear of getting his pristine walking boots muddy, a man who wanted to give the impression he had it all, when the truth was, materially we had very little. I often wondered why he would not hold my hand or show any affection towards me in public but it became increasingly obvious that he was a little ashamed of being seen with me. I did not fit his criteria; I refused to dress the way he thought I should dress. 'For fucks sake Hope, you look like a homeless hippie!' was one of his more complimentary comments. When we first met I thought he had found my style unusual and endearing but eventually I became aware that he was hell-bent on erasing any individualism I possessed. Inevitably I began withdrawing from our social life preferring to spend evenings crying alone rather that sit in a dark corner of some dingy clubhouse while he did his 'essential networking'. Colin was well liked and respected by many people who were won over by his charm. Colin the con man could talk his way out of trouble and into bed with anybody, including the wives of his associates. I never understood how he got away with that.

I have no idea why I stayed. Failure was quite a big issue with me, so I guess I was determined to make it work. I could say I made a huge mistake by staying but our son was the best thing that had ever happened to me, so all things for a reason.

After Ben was born, our lives settled for a while and I dared to think that family life would help to ground Colin, he seemed to enjoy being a hands-on father in the beginning but as with most things he soon tired of this when it was clear that Ben didn't share his fathers obsession with sport and the social life that came with it. Thankfully, Ben refused to be moulded into his father's ethic but when he started developing his own interests and strength of character around the age of ten, the cracks began to appear in their relationship.

I myself, had lost both of my parents within a short space of time when I was just 18 years old. It wasn't too much of a shock when my mother died as she had been ill for some while, but when my father collapsed barely two months later I was devastated. The doctors all said he had just given up, unable to carry on without his soul mate.

I found it so hard to come to terms with the fact that I had failed him; that he hadn't felt he could rely on me for support; but I think if I was totally honest I couldn't forgive him for not realising that I was barely an adult and I could have done with some guidance and support myself.

I made a decision that if I was ever lucky enough to start my own family, I would never let them down and I would always do my best to be there for them because feeling lost and alone is just about the worst feeling in the world.

Unfortunately, I always suspected that Colin would never feel lost without me.

So, for years I kept us together and I could not find the courage to leave, even though I knew it would have been better for all of us. In the end Colin, for once did the right thing and surprisingly, his final act of rejection completely shocked me.

Ben was fourteen years old at the time and the aftermath could have been a lot worse. After the initial, normal reactions of anger, shock, hurt and denial, his energies spent, he seemed to skip the teenage angst and rebellion years and soon became a protective adult. I was determined that father and son should try and maintain a relationship, so I was continuously instigating meetings between the two of them. I in turn kept up the pretence that it was an amicable split. Eventually, when Ben reached his 19th year, he told me that he was under no illusions about his father and that it was time for me to stop making excuses for him. 'Ma, he's *my* father and it's fine if he wants to make the effort to stay in touch; but I mean let's face it, I'm not sure if either of us can be arsed any more. It shouldn't feel this difficult.' I knew then, that if there was to be any form of contact between them, it would be on their own terms and with no input from me, which came as a huge relief.

So, in those last packing boxes were the final hurdles. I was still turning the cufflinks over and over in my hands when I realised that there was something else stuffed underneath the satin covered foam, another understated piece of jewellery, Colin's wedding ring; he had told me he had lost it but that he was 'sure it would turn up.'

With a brief sigh and the faintest ache in my heart, I whispered, 'Time to move on Cassie.' I quickly replaced every item into the box and marked it in large bold letters—FOR SALE OR CHARITY.

[9]

It's early March and moving day had arrived along with a last phone call from Jenny.

'May I just say Cassandra; I think you are making a terrible mistake. I just don't understand why you would want to leave when all your friends are here.'

'May *I* say Jen, nobody calls me Cassandra unless I'm being scolded!' No response, so I continue, 'will you be coming to wish me luck and wave me goodbye then?'

'Oh, I don't think so dear, I have a very busy day today, meetings to attend, people to visit and so on and so forth.'

Poor sods I thought. A short silence followed while *she* waited for my reaction and *I* waited for her blessing; neither of which were forthcoming.

'Well, I'll see you sometime Jen, maybe when I come to visit Lucy?'

'I don't have your new address or anything.' I felt that this was an excuse rather than a request; because I knew once you were outside Jenny's ten-mile radius her services were lost forever.

'I'll send you a New Address postcard from beautiful Brighton and Hove once I'm settled Jen.' Then as an after thought and to quell my pricking conscience I added, 'you're welcome to visit any time you fancy a day by the sea!'

'Well, that would be just lovely Cassa...Cassie, I may just do that, thank you so much.' I could tell by her gushing that she was relieved that we were ending the conversation on a positive note and I had to confess, I felt one more weight lifted as I placed the receiver down.

My final possessions hadn't warranted the hire of a removal van but Ben had enlisted the help of Matt who owned a reliable and robust estate car. It was a welcome sight when the boys arrived around mid-morning having left Cardiff at the crack of dawn. They brought with them croissants, coffee and a huge amount of enthusiasm which made me wonder how much caffeine they had already consumed on the journey down. Lucy and I had been busy transferring bags and boxes to her car so we were grateful for the impromptu breakfast. My dear, dear Lucy, the only person who was making me doubt my decision. As she stooped to squeeze one last carrier bag into the boot of her car she seemed very quiet and subdued. Instinctively, I put an arm around her shoulders and pulled her towards me, 'How will I survive without you Lucy?' My eyes were hot with the threat of tears so I quickly added, 'you had better come visit me...often.'

As she straightened up to face me I could see that she too was struggling to control her emotions.

'Girly weekends and seafront walks? Just try and stop me!' she gulped.

'Deffo!' Composure crisis averted.

'Cassie, you must be in absolutely no doubt that you are doing the right thing, just stop worrying about what everyone else thinks.'

We hugged each other and she added with a giggle, 'But do you know what scares me the most?'

'No, what?'

'I'm going to be Jen's next target!'

'Oh, Christ Lucy, I am so sorry!'

At that Ben and Matt came bounding over like two lolloping puppies.

'I think that was the last box—so are you ready ladies? Ma, your future awaits.' Ben gave a dramatic sweep of his hand towards the open road; my stomach gave a little flip. Ben casually rested his arm around my shoulders, 'Do you need to check inside before we go?' he added with a hint of concern.

I looked up at the tired house and handed the keys to Lucy, knowing that she would have a final search before depositing them at the Council Offices. 'No, I don't think so love, I'm good to go.' I realised I was actually shivering and I couldn't decide if it was fear of the unknown or just the shock of the finality of it all. Ben squeezed me a little tighter and then rubbed his hands together, 'Great! Well, lead the way Luce— we got ourselves a convoy!'

Matt let out a 'Yeeehah!' which stirred us all into action.

In that one single moment I had the living proof that all I needed was on that kerbside, right there and then. So, as I walked towards Lucy's car I did not look back once.

***

It had been a couple of weeks since I had last visited the flat; I had taken Ben to help me assemble some furniture and also for his honest opinion and hopeful seal of approval. It was a resounding success and he was visibly impressed and enamoured with not only my flat but also the whole building, so I was a little apprehensive that the magic may have worn off. I need not have worried, as soon as I unlocked the door to the main entrance hall, I felt it; the same sensation I had experienced on my first viewing. It was hard to describe, but it was almost like being in a cocoon, safe and tranquil.

Once the final box had been brought up to the flat and we were all sat amongst the happy disruption, the boys decided they would go off in search of provisions to bring back to the homestead for supper. Lucy let out a hefty sigh, 'Thank Christ there is a lift! Did you *have* to choose the second floor Cass?'

'My castle in the stars Luce.' I beamed.

'Not quite—there is someone above you.' She reminded me.

'This is very true, but the sky is huge and I'm willing to share!'

'Look at you,' she laughed, 'all stars and sea and sharing, you bloody happy hippy!'

It was true, I felt ridiculously happy, drunk on euphoria. We were both giggling at nothing in particular when the hunter-gatherers returned. They brought some excellent take away cuisine from the local vegetarian bistro and while I raided the packing boxes to find glasses and cutlery, the three of them set the table for the first supper in my new home. Later that night, after we had all found a place to lay down our sleeping bags along with our exhausted bodies, I found it difficult to sleep. There were varying degrees of snoring coming from all the rooms harmonising with the sound of the surf and it filled me with pure joy, I just could not stop smiling. I found myself thinking,

33

'I must not get too smug', but eventually the building calmed and lulled me into the best natural slumber I had experienced in a very long time.

[10]

A few days later when my band of helpers had finally left, I was sat on my tiny balcony overlooking the seafront, feeling somewhat surreal and very content.

It was a beautiful Spring-like morning and the sun was casting its' first warming rays through the French windows into my sitting room. The shafts of light were speckled with particles that looked like some magic stardust. Out to sea the water sparkled while the gulls hovered silently in an updraft; they looked like puppets attached to invisible wires as they stared intently into the depths waiting for breakfast to make an appearance. There were a few early morning body boarders making their way tentatively over the pebbles to launch themselves into the cool, calm ocean, and when each Neoprene clad body hit the water I shivered as they caught their first shock of breath.

'We are stardust, we are golden,' I started singing quietly to myself. 'I must tell Lucy the hippyitis is getting worse!'

I seemed to be suffering from sensory overload; I just could not feel negative about anything, not even when I tried to face up to the harsh realities. I had put everything I had into the move and paid four months rent up front. Add to that my insistence on putting my personal stamp on the whole place instead of listening to Lucy's sensible, 'bit by bit' advice; well in short, if I didn't find work by the end of the summer I was screwed. I had a brief moment of panic when I wondered if anyone would actually *want* to employ a forty-five year old Jill of all trades and mistress of none but it didn't seem to worry me for long. I was mystified as to where all the positive vibes were coming from. I picked up my coffee cup and The Argus classifieds in which I had circled a few job possibilities and stepped back into the warmth of my cosy sitting room, perhaps once inside I would feel a little less distracted.

Just as I was about to dial the first prospective job vacancy I was suddenly aware of a frantic scratching noise. Oh great, I knew it was all too good to be true, my perfect idyll must be rat infested! Although, they would have to be pretty hardy rats and possess some very impressive muscles to rattle the door with such vigour. I had already convinced myself that they were gnawing their way through three inches of solid wood door to get to me and therefore they must be some huge mutant breed. I armed myself with the baseball bat that I kept by my bedside, thankfully I had never had the need to use it in self-defence or in a sporting context; both scenarios could have ended badly one way or the other. I opened the door a fraction, leaving the security chain on (because of course this would prove to be an excellent rodent deterrent), peering down, gingerly I slid back the chain… 'Meeoww'

'Oooh, awh, hello sweetie,' I cooed, immediately melting with relief when I saw sat on my mat the proverbial cat. I guiltily disposed of the weapon and eased down into a not so elegant cat-stretch position to converse with my newfound friend. The feline responded positively by nudging my head and purring loudly.

'Well, aren't you a beauty? I'm not sure your stylist knew what they were doing when they gave you these highlights though.' I sympathised as I stroked the tortoise-shell fur, which was splattered with bright flecks of pink and duck egg blue.

'Who did this to you baby?' I sat back cross-legged and lifted the cat into my lap.

'I shall name you Magenta.' I announced.

'Picasso' a deep growl responded.

I lifted the animal to face me and eyed it incredulously, 'My god! That was amazing—how did you do that you clever girl?'

'His name is Picasso, on account of his ever-changing highlights.'

At this further explanation from a now distinctive Irish voice the cat leapt from my lap and began winding himself around the orator's legs in the way that cats only do with people they truly have an affinity with. The denim-clad legs were equally as colourful as Picasso's coat.

I jumped up, perhaps a little too quickly as it took me a few seconds to respond. There was a man in my doorway…yes, definitely a man standing there in my doorway.

'Oooh, ahhm, hello.' I was stupidly flustered.

Looking bemused, he proffered his hand and introduced himself, 'Hi, I'm Tom from upstairs and, this,' he said indicating to the cat, 'is Picasso—also from upstairs, he being the flatmate like.' He had dancing eyes this Tom, although as I was still gripping his hand I couldn't be sure whether this was a smile or a polite grimace. No, nice kind eyes, I thought and fervently hoped that I hadn't said that out loud.

'And you are--?' he gently coaxed, I had loosened my grip but I noticed that he still held my hand and I sprang back as if I had received an electric shock. What on earth was wrong with me?

'So sorry, I'm Cassie from this flat here—and I err don't have one. A cat that is...or a flatmate for that matter.'

'Well, Cassie from this flat here, it's a real pleasure to meet you. I do apologise if Picasso disturbed you but he likes to wander the halls when he gets bored with my company and of course he *had* heard that there was a new kid in the block.' At this he scooped an unresisting Picasso up into his arms and was turning to go when he added, 'It doesn't harm him you know?'

'What? Sorry?' I asked shaking my head slowly.

'The paint, it does him no harm...its non-toxic. Sure he's a grand lad as well as one of my best critics.'

I flushed a little as I reached out to stroke the cat's neck.

'That never even crossed my mind; he looks very content and happy.' I smiled feeling much more relaxed.

'Good—well then we'll leave you to it. We're all good people here Cassie, you've no cause to be afraid, we don't bite.' He smiled.

'Thank you that's good to know; nice to meet you both.' I gave Picasso one last stroke and said goodbye.

I closed the door gently and was suddenly overcome with unexpected emotion. I felt on the brink of tears but on the inside I was so calm that for once they didn't bubble over as they usually do. This was a new reaction for me and it took me a while to recognise what it was; it was the glorious feeling of being welcomed into a community.

[11]

After my meeting with 'the boys' from upstairs, there followed a busy two weeks. I was amazed that out of a handful of vacancies I had managed to procure four interviews, so I set about the task of hopefully securing a job. This gave me the opportunity to explore the area and the transport system in more depth. The fact that I didn't drive had often been met with a certain amount of scornful derision, and while it was true that having friends who were willing to offer the occasional taxi-service was always appreciated, it gave me such pleasure discovering different ways of getting from one place to another. I discovered that the Brighton I thought I knew so well was in-fact much bigger and even more warren-like than I had imagined. I spent hours making notes of landmarks, bus-routes and cycle paths and then transferred all my information onto a grid map that hung on my kitchen wall.

'It's like a scene from the bloody Great Escape' I laughed, relaying my escapades during a phone call to Ben.

'Ah, but you're loving this aren't you Ma?'

'Honestly? It's exhausting, but yes Ben I *am* loving it! I have discovered so many hidden gems as well as some 'interesting' areas that I perhaps won't choose to revisit. I just wish I could master boarding or roller-blading!'

'Don't even think about it...well not unless you have some lessons first.'

I imagined Ben raising his eyebrows and smiling in that 'I wouldn't put it past her' way. 'Hah, no worries there love. I'm pretty sure my insurance doesn't cover me for dangerous sporting activities.'

The jobs I had applied for were pretty varied but I hoped that their criteria would take into account my age and lack of experience, which seemed a contradiction in terms. I attended four interviews in one week, which was daunting and exhausting even though some were informal to say the least.

The bookshop in the centre of the busy main precinct practically begged me to start the next day but I didn't think for one minute that this was because of my impressive CV or indeed my interview skills. The interview had been conducted in a storeroom whilst I perched precariously on a pallet of books. The manager who could not have been a day over eighteen, explained how he was not dealing at all well with the stress of multiple deliveries of stock, 'Courtesy of the Universities reading lists for next Septembers new intake' he grumbled. He was eating a sandwich whilst talking to me and each time he took a bite he used the remainder to point to the various different skips, 'Two hundred copies of various Everyman's Poetry collections,' he paused to chew, 'in *each* skip…twelve skips to a pallet!' He shook his head in dramatic disbelief; his mouth was so full of sandwich and obvious contempt I thought he would choke. I told him that I was unable to start immediately but that I would contact him with a date as soon as possible; I didn't want to be too hasty.

The next interview was at a letting-agent further out by the Marina. This area had always struck me as a bit of a no-mans land kept alive by the Cinema and a large supermarket. I could hear the clock ticking and my stomach rumbling in the awkward silences that followed each question and I got the feeling that the manager had already made up his mind that I wasn't really the type that could be let loose on their exclusive customers.

My third interrogation was at a neat but very deplete library in the back streets of Hove and although it held a certain fascination, I could not imagine surviving there. I had visions of being discovered trapped in the alternative medicine section, my skin the colour of yellow parchment and adorned by cobwebs spun by the healthy arachnid clientele.

I was beginning to feel totally despondent and my confidence was at such a low ebb that I was tempted to retreat to my safe haven and not even attend my final appointment as I felt it was probably a little out of my comfort zone. It was a two –part interview for the position of assistant student liaison officer at the University of Brighton. I knew what a high standard was expected but I gritted my teeth and told myself that it would be good experience. This was the first 'serious' interview I had attended and although it was an intense two days, I felt I had given it my best shot. Forever the pessimist, I made a note of the plentiful retail and barissta jobs that were offering the minimum wage to Brighton's student population; if all else failed I would have to hop from job to job to make ends meet. I was very aware that we were creeping into April which would quickly be followed by the longer days and balmy nights so I was in danger of lapsing into holiday mode. I desperately needed to stay focused but decided to give myself two weeks for responses before letting panic set in, after all I had time-lined the end of the summer.

***

I had not had any further visits from our resident artist or his cat but heeding his comforting advice I was keen to introduce myself to the rest of the neighbours. I was determined to be as relaxed as possible so that I wouldn't repeat the gibbering performance that Tom had previously witnessed, so I chose a day when I had no further commitments, which didn't prove to be too difficult at that time. The nervous fluttering in my stomach betrayed me as I left the security of my second floor flat. One of the features of the building that I had immediately fallen in love with was the softly curved staircase that linked each floor. The warm oak banisters gave the impression of welcoming arms gently supporting all those who used them. I made a mental note to ask who was responsible for the impeccable upkeep of the communal areas and was immediately aware of my bicycle untidily propped against the wall in the hallway. I felt a sudden pang of guilt, 'Must do better Cassie.' I reprimanded myself. On the ground floor, I stood outside Flat One and squinted at the little name plaque, which emulated the one by the entry system at the main door.

'Uh-oh shit,' I whispered, 'Mal-ki-o-vitch.' I refrained from knocking straight away so that I could silently repeat the name to myself in the hope that I would avoid offending the occupant.

'Hi, Miss Mal-kee-ovitch?..Hello, Mr Malk—iovitch? Hey there, Mr and Mrs Malkiovitch?' For goodness sake Cassie get a grip; remember, 'we don't bite'. Tom's kind words and warm Irish brogue came to mind and gave me the courage to knock firmly on the door before taking a small step backwards and a large breath in. There was a spy-hole in the door and I suddenly felt strangely exposed, but not for long as I heard a series of

40

locks being methodically unlatched until eventually the door slowly opened to reveal an elderly lady. I hedged my bets, 'Mrs Malkiovitch?' I enquired gently. I was struck first by the colour of her eyes, so blue they were almost indigo, her hair was pure white and swept up into a gentle chignon, giving her an almost ethereal look.

'You must be Cassie,' she smiled warmly, 'please do come in, I'm Martha.' I detected a very slight American accent. As she stepped aside I noticed that while her physique was elegant and upright she was using a walking cane.

'Well, if you're absolutely sure,' I hesitated, 'but I don't understand, how did you know..?'

'Oh, inside information my dear.' She chuckled and tapped the side of her nose.

'Ahah, Flat 4, Tom and Picasso?' I smiled and she nodded in acknowledgement.

The layout of the flat was almost a mirror image of my own, so as I followed her through the short hallway and into the sitting room, I was momentarily taken aback by the comparison. Martha's décor was far more opulent than my own, with dark solid furniture and deep red velvet soft furnishings, as it was the ground floor; there was a large bay window where my balcony would be. The window was swathed in white voiles, letting in an arc of light, which prevented the room from feeling oppressive. In front of the window I noticed the dining table was set out beautifully for morning coffee.

'I am so sorry, I must be disturbing you, would you prefer it if I called back later?'

'Nonsense!' A voice shouted from the kitchen, 'We have more than two coffee cups and its real good Italian coffee...none of that Starlight Express rubbish!'

'He means Starbucks dear' Martha smiled apologetically, 'Cassie, this is my partner Melvin.'

***

Martha and Melvin, who from that day foreword, I would affectionately refer to as Em 'n Em, held my rapt attention (no pun intended) for the following two hours. They welcomed me with open arms and filled me with indeed the best Italian coffee and home baked muffins I had ever tasted. We exchanged

41

enough information about each other without it feeling intrusive. They had been together for almost fifty-seven years, having met during 1956 on a musical production of 'Damn Yankees' off Broadway. Melvin had been the musical director and Martha, a young dancer in the chorus line; this explained their elegant, theatrical demeanour. By the time the production had come to an end they knew they were destined to stay together and travelled the world treading the boards. 'Not all our shows were successes and we had some pretty lean times, but whatever the venue or type of audience, we gave it our all and had a helluva time in the process…being together was all that mattered!' Melvin told me enthusiastically, and then as though reading my thoughts he added, 'We never married for fear of breaking the spell.' They glanced at each other and the look that passed between them left me in no doubt of their adoration for each other.

'So, why Brighton?' I asked.

'We were just passing through and never quite got around to leaving,' Martha said matter of factly, 'Then when we walked into this building…well, something just happened, it was as if it had been waiting for us all those years.'

I took a sharp intake of breath before asking incredulously, 'You too?'

There was a twinkle in Melvin's eye when he squeezed Martha's hand.

'Yep, Martha believes there is a heart to this house that only attracts the right kind of people.'

'Now, Mel stop that nonsense and fetch Cassie her welcome gift please dear.' She gave him a playful push. Melvin jumped up, 'Of course Princess!' he said and gave a little bow before heading to the kitchen. I got the impression that he would go to the ends of the earth for Martha and that she would follow.

When Melvin reappeared he was carrying a beautiful basket containing a small potted lavender plant, a bag of the famous Italian coffee and four of Martha's delicious muffins, wrapped in cellophane and neatly tied with a beautiful red ribbon. I was so overcome I felt close to tears.

'Wow, what a thoughtful gift, thank you so much, I could not have asked for a warmer welcome!' I gulped and quickly regained my composure in time to add, ' I am hoping to have a small flat warming some time soon and it would make me so happy if you could come along, so look out for your invite!'

'We would be delighted dear,' Martha accepted on both their behalves, 'but please don't be a stranger in the mean time and if you need anything at all, don't hesitate to knock.' She added with a genuine smile.

Suddenly aware of the time, I prepared to leave the lovely Em'n Em in peace.

'So, should I be nervous about meeting the rest of the occupants?' I half joked.

'Not in the least my dear, although we see very little of Ray and Andy in Flat Two, they are a wonderful couple and I know they would be so pleased if you dropped by to say hello. You are more likely to catch up with them in the evenings as they both work all day. Of course you have already met the penthouse residents!'

Earlier, Martha had spoken about Tom with great affection while Melvin had nodded in agreement. I learned that after Toms arrival he had become a bit of a celebrity as the artist in residence and Picasso his sidekick had followed him home one day and refused to leave his side; there were times when Tom would return home to Ireland to visit his family, or take a trip away to exhibit his work and on these occasions he would entrust Picasso to Martha and Melvin, who appeared to relish the task. On his return, Tom would always stop by to share a drop of good Irish whiskey and tell them all about his trip. So my first impressions of his kindness had been right it seemed.

After thanking them once again for their hospitality I said my goodbyes and skipped up the stairway to my flat to drop off the welcome basket. As I placed the lavender on the balcony the heady scent blended with the fresh smell of the ocean and I decided to take a walk along the seafront towards Hove. This gave me time to enjoy the afternoon sun and the relaxed feeling that discovering my new friends had left me with. I was in no rush to get back but I was keen not to miss meeting with Ray and Andy, I was worried that it would break some kind of spell if I failed to make contact on that day, 'Maybe, I am just a little bit crazy' I thought to myself, but I decided that it actually wasn't such a bad way to feel.

[12]

As it happened I waited till the following afternoon to visit Flat Two. It was a Saturday and I thought maybe it would be a little less intrusive than waiting like some weird stalker for them to come back from work. I need not have worried about breaking any spells as they gave me the same enthusiastic welcome I had experienced from the rest of the residents. This flat was completely different in style and layout; there was a spiral staircase leading up to the bedrooms and bathroom, making it more of a maisonette; so they had utilised the space in a totally different way. The décor was very modern and minimalist and while not unpleasant it didn't quite have the cosy appeal that I loved, however, the occupants more than made up for that with their warm personalities. Ray had moved down from Yorkshire about 5 years ago and had bought the flat, using some money that he had inherited from an elderly Aunt,

'I loved this place as soon as I saw it and it is what kept me here for that first year. I was that homesick and had a couple of disastrous relationships in the first eight months, I was almost ready to bolt for home but Martha, Melvyn and Tom were so supportive and encouraged me to stay…and then I met Andy.' He smiled across at his partner. After being together for a year they had felt sure enough of their relationship to commit to living together.

'So, the trial period is over now and we plan to marry next year, if he can still put up with me that is!'

'Congratulations!' I smiled.

'Thanks,' Andy grinned, 'since I *have* learned to put up with him, it seems the decent thing to do; we are a bit old fashioned like that, unlike Martha and Melvin.' He winked knowingly.

'Well, whatever works, but quite ironic really.' Ray smiled.

It crossed my mind that this house and these people had a real pull on each other. It wasn't an uneasy feeling but more one of respect for the unknown power that seemed to be involved; I wish I knew where the source lay, was it in the building itself or the inhabitants… or maybe both.

'Can I get you a drink Cassie, you look like you could do with an early evening warmer' asked Andy, 'now let me guess, I think you might be a brandy and ginger girl?'

'Clever you,' I grinned, 'that would be lovely thanks.'

I discovered that Ray was the manager of a leading High Street bank and Andy worked as a landscape designer for a company based in Hove, they were hoping to eventually set up on their own, incorporating Andy's creativity and Ray's business acumen.

'Designing homes and gardens for the rich and famous!' gushed Andy as he returned with a tray of drinks and mixed nuts and olives.

I felt like I had know them forever, I was so comfortable in their company; there was that magic again, nothing had been damaged by my delaying our first meeting. Once more, Tom's name was mentioned in the highest regard, 'We are *very* fond of Tom, despite his blatant heterosexuality and his *enormous* artistic talent!' quipped Ray as they nudged each other and rolled their eyes upwards.

I mentioned that apart from Picasso's coat of many colours I had yet to witness this talent and they informed me that Tom had a small gallery on the seafront, which I should take a look at.

After drinks Andy and Ray took me through to the hallway to show me how to gain access to the courtyard garden at the rear of the building; I had been wondering what the extra key was for. I was surprised when on leaving their flat, we turned left, passing the staircase where I had propped my bike and on through a short passage way which led to an external door. Walking through this doorway was like stepping into a little oasis; the area was paved in herringbone terracotta tiles and adorned with beautiful potted displays of shrubs and plants. In the far right corner was a trickling water-feature that fed into a small pond scattered with water lilies and in the left corner there was a beautifully crafted wooden bench backed by a trellis that was covered in trailing white clematis. In the centre of the courtyard was a long wooden table and benches, which seemed to have been crafted from driftwood. As I absorbed the serenity of it all I was aware that I was being watched for my reaction by

Ray and Andy, 'this is just beautiful...all your design I presume?'

'Well, with a little help from the house.' Andy replied.

'Do you mean the house or the residents?'

'One and the same I guess.' He laughed.

I felt a little rush of happiness as I realised, that I was part of all this now.

'Everyone is free to use the courtyard whenever they like but we wanted to create something that could bring us all together now and then; we often have impromptu gatherings for drinks or a barbeque during the summer, so don't wait to be invited if you hear the clink of glasses!' said Ray.

'That's such a lovely idea; I'll listen out for that! Oh, and by the way I haven't set a date yet but it goes without saying that you are both invited to my flat warming.'

'We will look forward to that, thanks Cassie!'

Then with a touch of concern I added, 'Erm, just to warn you though, my idea of interior design is rather different to yours, so don't judge me too harshly.'

Andy looked horrified, 'Gawd, it would be just awful if everyone enjoyed the same taste...I can usually tell when I meet a person what sort of space they like to live in, it's a sort of extension of their personality.'

I could tell he was encouraging me to challenge his perceptiveness.

'*Surely* not after just one meeting?'

'You would be surprised.' Ray chipped in proudly.

'Go on then,' I playfully encouraged Andy, 'do your worst!'

Andy adopted a thoughtful stance with one finger pressed to his pursed lips and I struggled to suppress a giggle. Then tilting his head to one side and peering at me through half closed eyes he delivered his conclusion.

'Well, Miss Cassie, you strike me as a person who is very in tune with the universe and you possess a quietly spiritual side,' there was a sudden smothered snort from Ray as we glanced at each other but Andy persevered with just a hint of impatience, '*So*, I am imagining that your space will be very connected to the outside world. Lots of natural light, colours that reflect the ocean and the sky but also a touch of earthiness in there too.

47

Crystals, wind chimes, candles and Feng Shui are very important for your inner sanctuary. You love to be alone but at the same time you extend warmth to those people who are important to you. There is no room for insincere people in your life but it has taken you a long time to come to this point…dear Cassie, I cannot wait to see what you've done with the place!' he folded his arms to indicate the ending of his prediction. Ray broke into applause and was wearing a Cheshire Cat grin that conveyed 'I told you so'. My jaw must have dropped because he chucked me under the chin and said, 'Darling, as attractive as that look is, you need to take care you don't catch a fly!'

'Blimey Andy, are you sure you haven't got a sideline on the seafront? I asked astounded.

'What?'

'You know—a canvas booth with a sign out front, 'ASTRAL ANDY—CROSS HIS PALM WITH SILVER AND HE WILL DESIGN YOUR LIVING SPACE INSIDE AND OUT!'

We looked at each other and giggled which resulted in a gentle stream of banter although I had to admit that Andy had been pretty spot on with his prediction.

As we were making our way back into the house, I remembered why I had wanted to be shown outside in the first place; I had spotted a small ivy covered shed discreetly sited behind the open door.

'Oooh, do you think there would be room in there to fit my bike?'

'Thank god, we thought you would never ask!'

I took that as a reprimand for leaving my clutter in the hallway for far too long. Andy and Ray were going out for dinner that evening so with a hug from each of them that felt in no way over familiar, I promised that I would remove the offending article straight away and also that I would not forget to lock the door afterwards.

Opening the door to the shed I was met with a warm, earthy smell that threw me back to my childhood when my father had grown tomatoes in a small greenhouse in the backyard, I guessed this was emanating from the bags of potting compost that were stacked neatly along the wooden palettes to the right side of the shed. On this same side there was an ordered rack of gardening tools with a shelf above holding baskets of twine, plant food and seeds. It was all very precise and tidy and I had a little smile to myself thinking of Andy and how the words 'landscape design' were not exclusive to rich expansive grounds. I also noted that there was a very conveniently cleared space on the opposite side which I romantically mused had always been waiting for my bicycle and me, much like the rest of the house; or had Ray and Andy pre-empted my visit with a subtle hint, neither would surprise me. With the job done I shut the shed door and took a few moments to sit and enjoy the peace of the courtyard garden. I felt a different ambiance there than on my sea-view balcony, the surrounding sounds were muffled because of the high walls and abundance of foliage. It was like being transported from ocean to countryside in a few short steps, the birdsong was gentle and more spirited, compared to the plaintive sea-gull cry; I could barely make out the sound of the surf at all. Early butterflies danced around the buddleia and I could hear the gentle drone of bees making the most of the haven of nectar they had come across. Other buildings surrounded the courtyard but it was only truly overlooked by the kitchen windows of our own flats and I was happy to see that Martha and Melvin had direct access through the door leading from their kitchen, thus making up for their lack of balcony at the front of the building. I was aware of the muted rumble of conversations spilling over from adjoining gardens, along with the faint aroma of chicory and charcoal as people fired up their Saturday evening barbeques. It seemed the slightest hint of sunshine enticed everyone outdoors. Suddenly I realised how hungry I was, so I carefully locked the door to the secret oasis and climbed the stairs anticipating a glass of chilled wine to celebrate another successful day.

[13]

I awoke the next morning and went through the very strenuous in-bed stretch routine followed by my now daily mantra of 'just five more minutes'. The trouble was it seemed very easy to find an excuse to extend this to ten or fifteen more minutes; usually I reminded myself that hopefully this wouldn't be a permanent luxury and that I should just make the most of it, or in this case 'well it *is* Sunday after all.' A full hour later I was finally showered, dressed and drinking coffee whilst on the phone to Lucy.

'My god Cassie, you are getting so lazy! What happened to putting on your walking boots everyday and taking in the ocean air? You do realise that the sun won't always shine in Brighton don't you?'

Inwardly I actually found myself doubting that statement.

'Well, I know it sounds lazy to you Lucy but I just needed time to get to know the natives and settle myself in you know?'

'Hah, I think you settled within two seconds of entering that building!'

'Do I detect a slight hint of jealousy there Luce? Referring to my new abode as *that* building!' I teased.

'No, but you know what I mean, just don't get too complacent, you could lose it all before I have the chance to come and stay!'

Lucy was good at that, making the point tactfully but at the same time injecting a touch of humour.

'Seriously Lucy, I have been here almost a month now and the time is just drifting away like grains of sand.'

'On Brighton beach? You'll be lucky!'

'Ha, ha very droll. Listen seriously, I decided that I would wait until tomorrow to see if anyone gets back to me regarding the jobs I interviewed for and if not, then I will start the search again. If my money and luck start running out, then I may have to consider coming back to bunk with you after the summer.'

'Christ, I will come and help you look myself! Not because I would mind in the slightest if you came and stayed with me but I *truly* feel you should be there Cassie, I mean that.'

'You're on! I will be arranging the flat warming soon so I was hoping you would be able to come and stay for a few days...I would be a lot happier if my financial stability was sorted by then but if not we'll have to hit the situations vacant together; after all you helped me find this place, I feel you're under a certain obligation to make sure I stay!'

After my call to Lucy I attempted to get in touch with Ben, this was probably a bit ambitious as it was still only 10.30 am, so I left a message for him to call me back for a catch up that evening. As it was another lovely morning I decided that I would indeed take a walk, or an amble to be more precise, to take a look at the galleries and shops on the boardwalk. If I looked to the left of the building from my balcony I could view past the ever-diminishing skeleton of the West Pier, further on, the paddling pool and putting green and then onward to the boardwalk itself. This came to a halt at the huge, all singing, all dancing structure of the 'new' Brighton Palace Pier. I could appreciate the beauty in all of it and for that I had no explanation, although I was relieved that the house was nearer the West Pier. Scanning the front from my lookout I could see how the weekend crowds visibly diminished the nearer to Hove they got, the main hub swarming around the entrance to Palace Pier and the boardwalk, giving the illusion of the dot on a huge exclamation mark. A totally different vista from the one I was so privileged to witness at dusk when I would look out over the old pier and watch the exquisite dance of the starlings flocking together to create nature's art using the sunset as their canvas. Each time they swept through the sky they created a different brush-stroke, giving the harsh outline of the blackened ruins new life and a softness it lacked in daylight. There were times when the shapes they created seemed to mimic the shoals of fish that swam in the ocean below and then they would culminate into a giant whale or a leaping dolphin. I remembered thinking, if I saw that only once it would be something I would never forget...magical. I discovered from Martha that this

51

display was called a murmuration and I felt the word was so perfect.

I caught myself recalling my conversation with Lucy and I was left with no doubt that it would break my heart if I had to give up my castle in the sky. I quickly grabbed my bag and keys so that I could escape from any more negative thoughts and as I descended the stairs it seemed that each step gave me the reassurance I needed, so that by the time I reached the front door I felt my spirits lifted. I stepped out onto the pavement and stopped to listen to the sound of music drifting through the open window of Em and Em's sitting room; at first I thought they must be playing one of their collection of vinyl Broadway Hits, but when the piano stopped abruptly and they both dissolved into laughter, I realised that they were performing in exactly the same way as they had done for the past almost sixty years and still loving every minute of it. I made a mental note to see if they would consider letting me hear more.

I continued on till I could cross the busy Kings Road and take some steps down to the seafront, this way there was some protection from the traffic and I wouldn't miss out on the variety of sensory experiences you can only get in a seaside resort. Trying to distinguish between the busy chatter and delighted squeals of human beings and the screeching of the hungry gulls was difficult until I could hone in on each individual sound. There was an abundance of material for my favourite past-times of people watching and match the dog to its owner; this reminded me that I hadn't seen Tom or Picasso since our first meeting so I assumed that he was probably away and that his gallery would be closed. It didn't take me long to spot it amongst several others in the artists quarter, it was set back from the boardwalk and was small and unpretentious just as I had expected, the sign outside simply announced 'Tom's Gallery'. The full-length windows gave just enough of an insight to what lay within, tempting people to take a closer look. I was one such person and as I walked casually towards the doorway, I caught sight of Tom with his back to me. It felt a little disconcerting that I should in-fact recognise an almost total stranger from that angle. While my brain was trying to fathom this out, I was perhaps a little too preoccupied with taking in his tall, relaxed figure and the way at that moment, his arm was casually draped around the shoulders of a very attractive young woman; so preoccupied that I failed to see the 'PLEASE MIND THE STEP' notice until I was gliding past it with surprising ease and very little dignity.

'Aaagh, shit bloody stupid shit!!' I landed very noisily and awkwardly, wrenching my ankle.

In a matter of what must have been seconds but felt like an embarrassing eternity, I had added to my list of profanities and Tom and aforesaid stunner had spun round to survey my entrance to the gallery. My first ever tears since I moved to Brighton were then cascading down my face taking my 'natural look' make up with them, I suspect that it was both pain and a severe loss of dignity that brought this display on.

'Jaisus, Cassie,' he remembered my name, 'are you ok darlin'? he called me darlin'.

'Oh, Tom, I am so sorry…I was just passing—and I thought—that is I heard you had a—I just wanted to—and I was having such a lovely day as well. Oh, god—I don't mean--,' I was aware I was a blubbering wreck and that I was doing that awful sniffly, sobby thing that used to enrage Colin so much. I almost flinched, waiting for the inevitable degrading comments which he would always deliver in a manner that made me want to curl up and die. I was scared to look up, but suddenly Tom and 'stunner' were gently sitting me down onto a chair that had miraculously appeared and as if she was always prepared for such emergencies, she also produce a hot cup of tea and a bag of ice for my ankle.

'Jaisus Ailish, we have got to do something about that step before someone breaks their fecking neck!' Tom managed to be angry and sympathetic using one tone of his voice. Remarkable I thought.

'Did you put some sugar in the tea? She looks awful pale?'

I sipped the tea and was forced to look up as I gave a little shudder.

'As a sugar free drinker, I can safely say she has put *plenty* of sugar in the tea,' I wrinkled my nose in disgust, 'and don't worry too much about my pallor, I haven't acclimatized to the sea air just yet!'

I surprised myself by giving Ailish a little wink and I was rewarded with a smile and a sigh of relief, she was a beautiful looking girl with a mass of titian curls setting of her sparkling green eyes and aside from a little envy I found I liked her instantly. Tom was laughing and commenting on how he wasn't sure he could make the sign any bigger, but my attention had already been drawn to the work on display and before I knew it I had abandoned the chair and ice pack and was hobbling around the gallery.

'My god, Tom these are incredible.'

The incident had probably emptied the gallery but I no longer cared, I was happy to wander slowly from one exhibit to the next drinking in the amazing use of colour and light, 'reflecting nature' as Andy would have put it. They were mostly seascapes but all captured something very different.

'I feel a little inadequate amongst all this beauty, like the smallest, dullest pebble in a vast sparkling ocean.' I don't think I had intended to say that out loud but Tom had followed me around the gallery in silence and I was now aware of him by my side.

'That is probably the silliest *and* the sweetest critique I have ever heard.' He smiled down at me.

'Ah, a major fault of mine I'm afraid—saying the first thing that springs to mind. It gets me into a lot of trouble.' With my face burning I limped towards the chair to collect my abandoned bag and steady myself for a moment before leaving; I wanted to exit with a modicum of composure.

'Well Tom, this was lovely---well apart from the whole clown acrobatic thing of course!' I was desperately willing myself to stop talking and just go.

'Would you like me to give you a hand home?'

'No, no really, I'm just fine.' I gave Ailish a little wave and mouthed 'thank you' before managing to leave the building with the slightest of limps. The last I saw of Tom was his dancing eyes following me with a slight look of bemusement.

[14]

The following morning I had slight problems adhering to the wake, stretch and mantra routine. This was because the first thing I was aware of was a vague tapping sound which I automatically thought was rain on the window pane, I responded by pulling the duvet over my head. I liked the rain; I even liked walking in it, so why was my body not responding? Maybe it was because in my brain the gentle tapping had become an annoying buzz, culminating in a more urgent ring tone.

'Ring tone, ring tone, that's my phone, my phone….. that's my phone!' I leapt out of bed and although it was immediately apparent that there was something amiss with my ankle, I still proceeded to dance around in circles looking for the offending item.

'Ahah!' I pointed at the phone on my bedside table accusingly, then paused to take a few calming breaths before answering in what I hoped was a casual yet wide awake manner.

'Hello, Cassie Peters speaking.' So far so good.

'Ah, hello Miss Peters, so sorry to disturb you, it's Professor Bennett from Brighton University here.'

I gingerly sat myself back onto the bed, feeling strangely exposed, even though I was wearing perfectly respectable night attire…admittedly pale blue seahorse pyjamas with co-ordinated vest top were maybe not everyone's idea of elegance personified but they were damn comfortable. I could be professional if I was comfortable.

'Oh, hi there Professor, I hope you weren't waiting too long I was just er…just er watering the plants on my balcony…???*Christ Cassie, stay calm and think before you speak!*

'No, not at all dear. How lovely to have a balcony! Do you have a sea view?'

He wanted small talk, I could do small talk, and it would help to calm me. Maybe, that was his plan...pacify before crucify.

'I am indeed lucky enough to have a sea view, I was very fortunate to find my flat and I already feel very at home here.' I was running the risk of sounding too desperate and giving too much information away now we were on my favourite subject. Fortunately the professor continued, 'Well, that's marvellous because we would very much like you to join us here at the university as part of the student support team. That is if you're still available of course?'

There was a very slight pause while I tried to calm the smile that was slowly spreading across my face, 'That's wonderful news, thank you so much, I would be absolutely thrilled to accept!' Very professional I thought.

'You are most welcome Cassie; I am delighted to be able to offer you the post. Now, it will be confirmed in writing by the end of this week and you will be sent lots of information and formalities. Now of course the position you were interviewed for will not become vacant until the Autumn term, which begins in September, so I do hope that isn't too far ahead for you but perhaps it will give you some time to prepare and also to enjoy the summer! Of course you are most welcome to visit us as often as you like over the coming months and if you have any questions at all there will always be someone here to help.'

I was still beaming.

'I am sure there will be plenty of questions professor but I would quite like to come by the university at some point in any case, just to familiarise myself with some of the campus, if that's acceptable?'

'Absolutely, not a problem at all, I shall look forward to that. Perhaps if you could call beforehand and discuss with my secretary when would be a suitable time?'

'Of course, of course and thank you so much again Professor Bennett.'

'You're most welcome dear, goodbye for now.'

It felt like a long time after I put the receiver down that I stopped staring dreamily into space and hugging myself and then came a sudden rush of adrenaline when I just couldn't decide what to do first. I rang Ben who picked up immediately and said, 'Hey Ma, look I'm really sorry I didn't get back to you last night, we went to a gig and didn't get back till late. I am just about to go to a lecture so can we talk later?'

'Well, I guess in my new position as 'student support assistant', I shouldn't stop you from attending your lectures!' I grinned.

Ben was suitably impressed and delighted as was Lucy when I shared my news with her.

'It's official now Cassie, you are a resident of Brighton!'

'Party time!' I laughed.

After I had calmed myself down, I stepped into the shower and took some time to reflect on the last 24 hours. I remembered with acute embarrassment, the scenario at Tom's gallery, I think I may have even blushed at the memory of the way I felt when he had stood close to me. It was absurd. I mean, okay so he was very talented *and* seemingly a really nice bloke to boot; but then there was the lovely Ailish. I put it down to the fact that my emotions were all over the place, after all the last couple of months had been pretty full on. It probably hadn't helped that I had downed two very large glasses of wine and a couple of strong painkillers before collapsing into my bed the night before. Not a wise combination, no wonder I had slept so heavily, it was a good job that the rain had disturbed me enough so that I was partially awake when the telephone rang. Except...I hadn't noticed any rain on the windows, so what had that tapping noise been, someone knocking at the door maybe? Then the buzzing that had penetrated a little further into my consciousness, the doorbell perhaps? Once out of the shower I pulled on some jeans and a sweatshirt quickly to go and check if the postman had left any note for a missed delivery, but on opening my door the first thing I became aware of was the smell of freesias; they had been my mothers favourite flower because the light fresh fragrance reminded her of spring. There on my welcome mat was an A4 size package wrapped in plain brown paper and string, alongside the package lay a beautiful bouquet containing blue Delphiniums, purple Iris, white Roses and the violet blue freesia which were emitting the glorious scent. To my great surprise Picasso was sat patiently guarding the items, he immediately rushed to greet me half purring and half meowing in his excitement.

'What's all this about then matey?' I asked as I stroked his head gently. I picked up the flowers and package and Picasso quickly strode past me into the living room, confident that he was welcome. I laid the flowers on my dining table and bent briefly to inhale their sweet aroma before sitting on the sofa to unwrap the parcel. Tucked inside the string, which Picasso was eagerly waiting to pounce on, was a small business card from Tom's gallery, I nervously removed it and flipped it over.

For Cassie
A welcome gift for our new neighbour
There are no strangers here, only friends you've yet to meet.
Tom and Picasso

I recognised the words immediately as a quote from the Irish poet William Butler Yeats. I could feel the threat of tears, because with those few short lines Tom had shown that he understood how mortified I had felt that day at the gallery and how important it was for me to be accepted. I glanced down at Picasso who was now relaxing next to me on the sofa, 'Your flatmate is an exceptionally nice man.' The cat slanted his eyes and purred loudly in agreement. I carefully removed the paper from the parcel but could scarcely catch my breath when I revealed the most amazing painting of the West Pier at sunset, complete with my dancing murmuration of starlings. Once again I was struck by the use of colour but also the attention to detail, each tiny soaring bird seeming to be a portrait in itself. I was stunned that he would give me such a gift. I took the picture and still trembling slightly I propped it against some books until I could decide where it would be shown at its best; I found a vase to put the flowers in and placed them at the centre of my dining table. I felt dazed but not in a bad way and had it been a few hours later I would have felt inclined to have a glass of brandy. It took me a few moments to gather my emotions, then I placed Tom's card in my diary for safekeeping and scooping the cat up in my arms I hobbled up to the next floor. Standing outside Flat four, I suddenly realised that I had never actually visited this level of the building and Tom's was the only flat I hadn't seen, it was a little unnerving. Picasso immediately jumped out of my arms and ran back down the stairs, so after knocking on the door a few times I guessed there was nobody home. I found the cat had plonked himself outside Em and Em's so I decided to seek out a bit of company. After the obligatory 2 minutes of locks and chains being unlatched, Martha's calming face appeared at the door, 'Cassie, how lovely to see you, please do come in, oh and you've brought monsieur chat with you—come,' she was struggling to hold the door and beckon us in at the same time and I was afraid that the cat would trip her up as he was busy nuzzling her ankles, 'Mel honey, put some coffee on, Cassie is here—and Picasso too!'

***

Ten minutes later with the smell of fresh coffee and homemade blueberry muffins wafting from the kitchen, I suddenly realised that apart from the hastily consumed wine and painkillers, nothing had passed my lips since the previous afternoon. I had plonked myself at the table in expectation of sustenance, then realising how rude this must have seemed I asked if I could help get the tablemats for Martha.

'No dear, that's just fine, you sit right there, you look exhausted!'

'Oh, that obvious huh?' I asked grinning. I suddenly noticed that Martha seemed much steadier on her feet and was not relying on her stick.

'Hey Martha, you're not using your cane!'

'Ah, yes well thankfully I do have periods when I feel a lot stronger and I make the most of getting rid of that wretched appendage!' she smiled mischievously whilst nodding to the stick propped against the side-board. I had never asked why she used the cane and now didn't seem appropriate, especially as Melvin appeared with a tray overflowing with deliciousness.

'My word Cassie, you look worn out; here let me pour your coffee honey while you tell us what's been going on!'

I noticed that Picasso was already near the kitchen doorway wolfing down a bowl of cat food. 'I hope you're going to let Tom know his cat is pigging out. At this rate neither of us will make it out of your door!' I laughed.

'Oh, no it's alright dear, monsieur Picasso is our guest for a few days while Tom is away in Ireland, so we can spoil him just a tad, I usually treat him to a little grooming while he's here, it keeps the coat of many colours toned down a little.' Even though Martha had whispered this information, clever Picasso disappeared rapidly out of the back door and into the courtyard. I was disappointed that I had missed Tom and angry that I had not been awake when he had called, but quickly took comfort in the fact that at least he hadn't witnessed my morning after look.

Once my hunger had been sated, I began to relay the events of the last few days to Em and Em, starting with my delightful meeting with Ray and Andy, then onto the disaster in the gallery and concluding with the adventures of that morning. Mel poured more coffee and shook his head in amusement; 'You sure don't do things by halves Cassie!'

Martha was giggling delicately and dabbing her eyes, which were alive with merriment, 'And you certainly know how to deliver a good story darling!'

'Well,' I said sheepishly, 'I'm glad I can keep you both suitably entertained! Of course you do realise that I am now destined to stay...in the house I mean?' I looked from one to the other as they raised their mugs of coffee and without any prompting they toasted in unison, 'So everything is as it should be!'

I will never be able to describe how their obvious delight made me feel, but knowing I had contributed in some small way was reward enough.

***

It was past one o'clock before I managed to extricate myself from the comfort of Em and Em's company. When I had questioned them about the music I had heard the previous day they proceeded to deliver an enthusiastic rendition of 'I'm a Yankee Doodle Dandy.' I could hardly believe how clear and precise their voices were and so impressed by the performance that I applauded and whistled loudly for more. Melvin obliged by playing 'Rhapsody in Blue' on the piano. I could only watch in awe as the years drifted away from their faces and how Martha elegantly swayed to the music that so obviously touched her soul. It was a strong reminder of how important it is to keep good memories alive.

As I was leaving I told them that the invites for the flat warming would be going out shortly and that I hoped it would take place the following weekend, providing that it suited everyone. Martha clasped her hands together in excitement at the prospect of meeting Ben and my friend Lucy who they had heard so much about.

A little later in the afternoon I wandered into town to do some shopping, I felt incredibly satisfied with the course my new life was taking.

'And it's all thanks to that lovely building,' I thought to myself, 'my little house of hope...now that *is* ironic...maybe mum and dad *are* looking out for me after all! As I walked back along the board-walk, I thought I would visit the gallery to thank Ailish for her kindness the day before. The shutters were closed and when I enquired next door, I was told Ailish was in Ireland. Of course she was. Strangely, it didn't seem to matter so much any more, so I went home to start the plans for my party.

[15]

Having made sure that both Ben and Lucy would be free the following weekend I posted invites to the rest of the house. It was going to be such a small gathering that at first I worried in case someone couldn't make it; but then Ben had asked if he could bring Kate, as well as Mathew and Alice to stay over on the Saturday night.

'That would be lovely Ben; they are most welcome! I assume that you and Kate would like the spare room?' I enquired tentatively. I had learnt never to presume anything.

'If you're cool with that Ma, thanks.' I could almost sense his slight embarrassment 'Would you like Matt to bring an airbed or anything?'

'No, I think I have the sleeping arrangements covered, Lucy can bunk in with me, you and Kate in the second bedroom and don't forget I have a sofa-bed in the sitting room; maybe if Matt could bring a sleeping bag and a couple of pillows just in case.'

'Awh, that's great Ma, we're all really looking forward to it. See you around lunchtime on Saturday!'

Lucy was going to come on the Thursday so that we could have a bit of quality catch up time before the weekend and of course I would be roping her in to help me out.

When I woke on Wednesday, I realised that it was the first time I didn't actually have anything planned, so I hauled on my walking boots and decided to head for the South Downs Way; it felt good to relax and start enjoying some of my old hiking turf.

The unpredictable English weather had never deterred me from enjoying our glorious landscape; its diversity provided ever-changing vistas that never failed to fill my heart and soul with pure joy. Obviously, for walking purposes it was preferable if I wasn't caught in the middle of a raging storm but a little rain and a breeze could prove just as exhilarating as a clear blue sky.

I packed a small rucksack with all the usual requirements, a first-aid pouch, a bottle of water, a sandwich and fruit, a small amount of money, spare socks and an Explorer map. I smiled to myself as I remembered how Lucy was fond of telling people that I prepared for a major expedition even if I was going to post a letter. The map was also a source of amusement because we very often chose to walk blindly, following our instinct and going off route, in-fact it was only recently that we had invested in a compass. Considering the places we had been, we were pretty lucky not to have had a search party out at any point on our adventures.

The first time Lucy and I had decided to take strolling to a different level was after the boys had flown their respective nests and we were suddenly aware of the void in our lives; we booked a weeks holiday on the Isle of Skye to commiserate with each other but little did we know how much it would broaden our horizons. We hadn't gone prepared for the discomforts that inevitably occur when novices take on a serious scramble in the Black Cuillin mountains; but reaching the top of McLeod's Table shouting 'FREEDOM!' and giggling as if we were high on laughing gas made up for all the sweat and blisters. That was when we realised how liberating and energising a strenuous walk could be and we vowed there and then to get kitted out properly and plan some long distance trails. After Skye we spent many free weekends walking the South and North Downs way, we also took a couple of short breaks in Cornwall to explore the South Coast Path; but last year had been the main event. We completed Wainwrights coast to coast, walking 197 miles across England in two weeks, an unforgettable experience that quite literally had changed my life. It was the first time that I acknowledged the fact that I had an inner strength which I didn't know existed but also a restlessness which had not left me until the moment I had walked through the door of my Brighton home; it had been a painful journey but I felt at last I had arrived. Checking the battery on my phone, I grabbed my keys and headed out. It was a good day for walking, there was a slight breeze hurrying the scanty clouds across the sun, but knowing how fickle the elements could be I set out at a pace that would ensure a pleasant couple of hours before lunch time.

I crossed the road directly outside the house and was soon onto the first shelf of pebbles. I stopped briefly and watched two laughing dogs causing havoc chasing the seagulls. Failing to impress their owners they proceeded to have a tug of war with a huge piece of bladder wrack seaweed, nature's bubble-wrap, pretty soon both humans and canines were racing around with infectious hilarity.

Determined not to be distracted by the entertainment I carried on past the Fishing Museum and on towards the Artists Quarter; I resisted the temptation to mooch around the stalls displaying colourful handcrafted jewellery and scarves and a quick glance towards Toms Gallery confirmed that it was still closed for business…so no distraction there either. There is a small freeze frame section just past the Artists quarter where the boardwalk becomes home to an almost 'kiss me quick' era, bordering on tacky but not failing in its attack on the senses. The sound of the end of Pier amusement arcade and rides become an aural assault after nature's dulcet tones; while the cloying scent of fish, chips, doughnuts and candyfloss are so heady, the need of a snorkel and flippers wouldn't seem out of place to wade through the heavy atmosphere.

A few yards past the pier, I came up for air and with some relief I welcomed the return of the refreshing ocean spray. I increased my pace and soon I reached Rottingdean where I crossed the busy road to take the path towards the South Downs Way, keeping the impressive structure of Roedean Girls School to my right. In what seemed no time at all I was walking along a beautiful swathe of green scattered with vibrant yellow Gorse with its natural sweet coconut-vanilla scent that immediately lifted my spirits. The sound of the surf and seagulls was replaced by the warbling swifts as they swooped into their own ocean of grass and shrubs. I was reminded of the house and its two halves. I found a peaceful spot to have my lunch and reflect on all that had happened over the past months and although it all still seemed a little unbelievable, I was beginning to lose the nagging doubts that life was just a little *too* good. Maybe it was just my time and fate had led me to this happy place I found myself in now. I lost track of how long I sat there, but when I stood and gathered up my backpack and my thoughts, it was the most natural and comfortable feeling to turn towards the sea and home.

[16]

Lucy arrived on Thursday as planned, just in time for breakfast on the balcony.

'Yum strawberries and yoghurt, the perfect accompaniment for my contribution to breakfast,' she laughed as she produced a bottle of Bucks Fizz from a cooler bag.

'Hah! Just as well we have coffee and croissants to follow' I grinned, 'it's so lovely to have you here darlin.' I gave her a big hug before fetching the glasses from the kitchen. We started breakfast at 9.00 and we were still sat there with our coffee at 11.00, there was so much to catch up on and it seemed a lifetime since we last had such a good in depth conversation. I had been worried that because my life had gone through so many changes in such a short space of time the chat would be a little one sided but thankfully Lucy had lots to tell me about too. William, her youngest was back from travelling and although Lucy would never say, I think she was hugely relieved to have him back home and the fact that he was looking to settle for a while at least, gave her some inner peace. Stephen, her oldest son had been in a serious relationship for some time and there was talk of an imminent wedding.

'That's great news Lucy, lots to keep you occupied then!' I laughed, but noticed her body stiffen a little. I gave her a questioning look. 'What?' She scanned the ocean as if searching for inspiration. I jumped up from my seat and was at her side kneeling next to her, 'Lucy, what is it, are you ill? Is it the boys? Please darlin' I know there is something your not telling me.' I pleaded with her.

'Do you know, you have called me darlin' twice since I got here? Now where would you have heard that endearing expression I wonder?' her lip twitched and I flushed to my roots. 'I don't know what you mean,' I protested, 'and anyway, stop changing the subject.'

Lucy turned to face me and took both my hands, I noticed her eyes were twinkling…she didn't look sick.

65

'Cass, you know you would be the first person I would tell if I had any problems, which incidentally I don't.' Relief washed over me. 'There are just some things that need to be left unsaid until the time is right. Now please get up off your knees before I give you a knighthood.'

As I stood and looked down at her, I recognised something in her face and realisation suddenly struck me, 'Oh my god Lucy...you've met someone! Who, when, where?' I was jumping up and down and clapping my hands in glee.

'See, this reaction is precisely the reason I wanted to keep it to myself for a while. It's too soon Cass, too fragile even to share with my closest friend, and I *know* you understand what I mean...darlin'. This last comment was delivered with such an exaggerated Irish accent and a mischievous grin that I laughed out loud and we both giggled a little self consciously.

That's how we left it, both of us realising that indeed some things are too personal to share until they have had time to settle into your own being. We decided that a walk was in order, so while Lucy unpacked, I cleared the remnants of our breakfast and prepared for another trip over the South Downs.

The following day we kept busy combining shopping with sampling different coffee shops. In the evening I had a quick clean around the flat and prepared the sleeping arrangements as best I could, we had dinner in the garden which Lucy described as a 'hidden oasis'. I had hoped that we may be joined by Em 'n Em at the least, but I knew they would feel it was an intrusion unless invited and though the thought crossed my mind I didn't want to tire them for the next evening. Also, as Lucy pointed out it still got chilly quite quickly.

Later as we sipped an Irish coffee on the balcony I had an anxious feeling.

'Blimey Lucy, what if no one turns up tomorrow?'

'Well, I'm here...what more could you want?'

I could always rely on Lucy to make me smile but that night I lay awake pondering on the different scenarios and excuses that could be used for not attending my little gathering. Em 'n Em might be so full of home made muffins that they couldn't climb the stairs and of course the lift had a weight limit. Ray and Andy got a call from a client who insisted that their garden should be landscaped by the light of a full moon. Tom and Ailish had decided to get married while they were with all the family in Ireland... 'Sure, there wouldn't be room for them all to stay here darlin'.

I finally drew the line when I started imagining Ben saying he had way too much studying to do to party. Instead I concentrated on the calm of the home I was rapidly getting used to and within moments I was fast asleep.

***

[17]

The following morning all doubts dissolved with the arrival of Ben and his entourage. I had just begun preparing breakfast while Lucy was taking a shower when I received a text from Ben,

'E.T.A 15 MINS.   PUT KETTLE ON...ANYTHING NEEDED?'

'JUST YOUR SAFE ARRIVAL X' which was my standard reply.

If nothing else Ben was always reliable, he could sleep through a thunder storm if he didn't need to be anywhere but if he made a promise to be there then there he would be. Lucy appeared and spying the extra caftiere and crockery she smiled, 'Bens on his way then?'

'Yep, good job we got supplies yesterday.'

The sudden influx of noise and energy into the flat was a shock but not unwelcome and by the time we had demolished fruit, cheese, croissant and coffee it was almost midday. I suggested that while the weather was good we should take a stroll into Hove to refresh us all before the main event.

We walked along the promenade all the way to Hove Lagoon, a small boating lake within a park. It was a relaxed walk and a great opportunity to chat resulting in a kind of relay where we all swapped places along the way taking up the baton where the last person had left the conversation. Eventually Ben and I dropped to the back of the group and he took my arm and linked it through his, 'Ma, you look amazing.'

'What are you after?'

'Jesus, I'm just saying...' he laughed, 'seriously you look really...different.'

I frowned, 'How do you mean?'

'I can't remember seeing you so at peace with yourself for a very long time.'

A huge wave of guilt swept over me and I stopped and turned to face him.

'Has it been that bad love...I am so sorry.'

'Ah but I see you have yet to master the art of accepting a compliment without self-deprecation grasshopper.'

I grinned, 'Smart arse.'

'It makes me happy ma.'

'What, being a smart arse?'

'Well there is that.'

I squeezed his arm in acknowledgement as we walked on.

'I like Kate.'

'Good. So do I.' he grinned.

It was a good feeling to acknowledge that we were both happy with each others current situation.

Back at the flat there was no time to worry about the arrival of guests as we all pitched in and set out the food and drinks we had prepared for the evening.

Unsurprisingly, first to arrive at precisely seven o'clock were Melvin and Martha. I greeted them both with a gentle hug and a kiss but I was conscious of Martha's frailty and led her to a tub chair which I thought would be suitably supportive and comfortable, but she dismissed this with a wave of her hand, 'Not before I have had a guided tour from your young Ben!' she smiled, her blue eyes twinkling with merriment.

Ben was more than happy to introduce everyone and when he slipped Martha's arm in his to show her around the flat, I noticed Melvyn followed closely but not so close that she couldn't enjoy her moment.

Andy and Ray were next to arrive and as Lucy commented later, they were like a mobile party in themselves, a complete double act brimming with banter and one liners but at the same time listening intently and politely to what everyone else had to say. 'So Andy, is my space as you expected?' I asked tentatively seeking approval.

'Darling, it is so much more! Extremely tasteful in its own bohemian way and so very you!' Ray stood beside him grinning and nodding in agreement so I guessed that was as close to a compliment that I was going to get. I went into the kitchen to open a bottle of wine and when I returned to the sitting room the guests were gathered around Tom's painting which I had decided to hang to the left of the balcony doors above my small writing desk, 'I hung it here so that the changing natural light in the room enhances the colours at different times of the day.' I explained.

'This has to be one of Thomas's.' commented Martha with a pride in her voice that sounded almost maternal.

'Yes,' I blushed, 'an extremely generous house warming gift…I just hope I have done it justice placing it there.'

'Sure you have a good eye. It looks grand where it is.'

At the sound of Toms voice I felt the heat of the blush increase, everyone turned at once to face him and I fervently hoped that this would detract from my flustered look.

Martha had opened her arms and was enveloping him in a hug as he glanced at me over her shoulder and said, 'Sorry, I did knock but the door was ajar so we let ourselves in.'

'No problem at all! Ailish hello again, I am so pleased you could make it! Now what can I get you guys to drink?' I was relieved to escape to the kitchen to give myself a telling off for getting myself into such a flap but was unable to avoid the radar of Lucy's lifelong honing skills. To her credit she only whispered, 'Now I understand.' She smiled knowingly. 'Well I'm glad you do 'cos I sure as hell don't! Come on, help me put some more grub out…supplies are getting low out there.' I quickly diverted the conversation and headed for the gentle buzz of the guests who were getting on just fine without me in my sitting room. Tom was explaining to Ben and Kate the fact that he only ever used Belgian linen for his canvas as it was the best of all linens, 'Much easier to work with than cotton canvas because the threads are finer and the weave is tighter so once stretched and primed it's less likely to distort or shrink.'

'Jaisus, you'll be sorry you asked that question!' Ailish interrupted with a soft giggle. Tom smiled, 'Well sure, that was the short answer!'

Meanwhile, Martha and Melvyn had a captive audience with Matt and Alice as they shared their love of musical theatre and the way it had shaped their lives. Ray and Andy were hovering between the two conversations contributing snippets of information and seemingly enjoying the whole ambiance. Lucy brushed past me with a tray of drinks; I had no idea when she had taken that task away from me. I was aware that I was having another 'bubble moment' where everything was being captured in one freeze frame, this sensation wasn't new to me anymore and therefore had ceased to faze me. I just rode with it and absorbed all that was happening around me and although it seemed to last forever it must have been a matter of seconds before everything snapped back into place. I picked up a wine glass and gently tapped the side with a spoon to get everyone's attention, Tom was the first to look up and he touched Ailish on her shoulder which caused a ripple affect across the room as the conversation slowly ebbed away.

'Don't look so worried Ben; I am not going interrupt drinking time or embarrass you... too much,' I smiled over at him and he raised his eyebrows as if that was a common occurrence. ' I just wanted to thank you all so much for being here, it means a lot to me to bring together all the special people in my life, past and present. I could not have made this part of my journey without a single one of you.' There was a hushed silence and I think I may have heard a gulp and a sniff coming from Lucy's direction, I raised my glass and continued, 'So I will just say, *May the roof above us never fall in and may friends gathered below it never fall out! Slainte!'*

The room erupted with resounding shouts of Cheers and Slainte and I heard Martha saying, 'How wonderful!' but I was mostly aware of Tom, on the other side of the room with his warm smile and his laughing eyes, raising his glass to me and tilting his head in acknowledgement, that I had chosen an old Irish proverb almost as a personal thank you.

I think it was Melvin who suggested we all transfer to the courtyard to enjoy the remainder of the evening outside, although I think his ulterior motive was to let Martha rest on their sofa. The party formed a kind of conga line each person taking a selection of food and drink to the beautiful outside space. The sky was the colour of a blood orange casting an exquisite warm glow across the area, Melvin opened up the door to their flat and disappeared to provide us first with a gentle piano recital and then later with a tray of coffee and tea.

'Thank you so much Mel, this is lovely...is Martha ok?'

'Just a little tired is all,' he smiled, 'it's a long time since we partied!'

'Shall I take her in some tea?' I asked, still not convinced.

71

'I think some one may have beaten you to it' he chuckled as he nodded towards the door, 'she's a very popular lady… my Princess!'

I looked up in time to see Tom disappearing through the door carrying a tray, Melvin was smiling now but he too looked tired. I began to gather the plates and glasses up as a signal to everyone else that it was time to bring the lovely evening to an end. I told Melvin that I would pop in and see them very soon and to give Martha a hug from me, this meant I had to hug him twice which made him laugh. As we all tumbled into the hallway and said our goodbyes for the night I felt happy that the party had gone well but I couldn't help thinking about M 'n M and their love for each other and how I wished I had known them longer. Lucy and the others were ahead of me as we climbed the stairs, then I heard Tom saying, 'Lock the door after me Mel, but be sure and call me now ..you know it doesn't matter the time.'

'Of course Tom you know I will, but you know she had a wonderful evening and she will be fine after a rest.'

I stood stock still on the stairs till he reached me.

'Cassie, are you ok, you look like you've seen a ghost?'

I couldn't explain to him the feeling that had reached me on the stairs, because I didn't understand it myself, a mixture of fear and sadness, almost like I was losing something very dear to me.

'Martha…is she ok?'

'I'm sure she'll be just grand,' he answered, 'she said to tell you what a lovely time she had and that she was sorry she was such a party pooper!'

'Bless her, she stole the show!'

There followed a moment that seemed much longer than it probably was and then we both pointed in the direction of our respective flats and muttered something about getting back to the people in them.

Once inside my flat I was relieved to feel the warmth returning to my being as I was greeted by the sounds of Lucy singing in the kitchen as she washed the dishes and the kids discussing what their favourite party games were.

'Hey Ma, you up for a game of Trivial Pursuit?

'Sounds great, but I'll just give Lucy a hand first.'

Later, as we were finishing off the last game before going to our beds, the evening was discussed and deemed a success. The diversity of my neighbours was greeted with great enthusiasm.

'Yeah, there is a really eclectic mix of characters here ma, no wonder you fit in so well!'

'Cheeky bugger' I smacked Ben playfully.

'Yeah, and Tom's niece is really cool too.' Matt said while Alice nodded in agreement.

'Niece?'

'Yeah, Ailish, nice name too' smiled Alice.

'Niece?' I repeated.

'Yeah ma, you know, as in daughter of a sibling?' snorted Ben.

'N..n..n'

Lucies hand shot out to take my arm, 'Please don't repeat yourself Cass.'

Ben looked at me and burst into laughter, 'Ha-ha, I know what you thought you nutter!'

He was shaking his head in disbelief while I blushed with embarrassment and rounded off the evening's entertainment.

'Shut up you lot.'

As I lay in bed listening to the musical snoring of my house guests, it occurred to me that it had never crossed my mind that Tom and Ailish were *related* rather than being *in* a relationship.

'Now what?' I whispered to myself.

I swear the house responded with a calming sigh.

[18]

The following morning, once my guests had eventually emerged and waited patiently in line to use the bathroom, it was agreed that a short walk and brunch in town would be a pleasant way to conclude the weekend. There was a briskness to the air that soon saw us heading inland to the warmth of the Lanes where we found a cosy café to gather in. While we sat waiting to be served, it occurred to me that I felt I had completed a long journey which had begun way before the decision to relocate to Brighton and that at last I felt able to relax in the knowledge that for now I was secure. I was ready to give time and myself to other people again; I had missed that so much. Unsurprisingly, it transpired that although the University term was only part way through, Ben, Kate, Matt and Alice were already discussing looking for a house to share between the four of them. They were feeling confined in the present house and wanted something that resembled a proper home.

'That's fantastic news!' I cried hugging each of them in turn, 'You have no idea how happy that makes me!'

Ben was beaming at me with relief, 'I didn't think you would be too sad to see the back of Joe,' he shook his head 'Christ knows where he will end up!'

'Oh I'm sure he'll muddle through,' I smiled weakly 'with a little help from his parents and like minded people…every one finds their niche eventually.'

There followed a moments silence as though we were all contemplating where Joe's lifestyle would actually lead him.

'Oh, but what about Graham, I haven't asked after him for so long!'

'Christ, sorry I forgot to tell you ma, Graham has already moved out. Yeah, he got himself a lovely little flat and is sharing with a mate who is on the same course. It's around the area that we are looking at, so hopefully we will be close by.'

The conversation about impending exam results and university life continued through brunch. It felt good to discuss Bens' future plans without worrying about my own, so when we came to leave the cafe I was a little sad that I couldn't have a bit longer to chat with him. As if reading my thoughts Ben put his arm around my shoulder, 'This has been a great weekend Ma, but we will fix a date for me to pop down on my own soon, yeah?'

'Awh that would be great, before I start work in September or maybe I could come to you if you get a new place sorted?'

'Or both!' he winked.

It was gone three o'clock when they left and Lucy and I made our way back to the flat to collect her bags before she too set off home. I suddenly felt a slight panic as I walked her to her car, 'Lucy...I won't lose you will I?' I asked with a hint of a tremor in my voice. She looked at me in astonishment, 'My god Cassie...you still can't grasp it can you? Whatever happens in life, however much our circumstances change wherever we both end up, nothing will ever alter our friendship...you will never lose me...I hope you feel the same way?'

'There is no doubt about that! I was just checking... you know before you head off.'

'Yeah, well next time I come maybe we can discuss why you feel the need to check?'

It was then that I knew for certain Lucy was waiting for the right moment to share something with me.

I walked home the long way round, going further into town so that I could walk up Church Street where I knew there was a stall selling beautiful fresh flowers. It would probably blow my budget but I wanted to get something special for Martha. There was a huge choice but I chose a beautiful bouquet of spring blooms in whites and yellows because they looked like sunshine.

'Everyone deserves a bit of sunshine in their lives.' I commented taking them from the flower seller who nodded in bemused agreement.

As I walked back towards the seafront I spotted a tiny dark cloud on the horizon, my body shuddered for the briefest of moments, then when I looked up it was gone and although the anxious feeling subsided I felt my pace pick up the nearer I got to Sanctuary House. I practically ran up the steps and was breathing heavily as I entered the hallway, 'Must organise my exercise routine' I panted to myself. I felt a bit foolish knocking on Em'n Em's door in such an urgent manner but when it was Mel who appeared I felt slightly concerned, as it was unusual not to be greeted by Martha.

'Oh…oh hi Mel,' I said, trying hard to conceal my worry, 'I just thought I would pop by to see how Martha is feeling today…I brought flowers…but if she's resting perhaps you could…' I stopped when I saw his gentle smile as he opened the door wider to welcome me in.

'Cassie come in, come in my darling girl!' I heard Martha calling from the sitting room and Mel, forever the gentleman gestured for me to go ahead of him down the hallway. Martha was reclining on the sofa supported by several plump cushions and cocooned in a large blanket. Whatever darkness had been on the horizon had disappeared, rays of sunshine were finding their way through the curtains and coming to rest upon Martha giving extra warmth to her frail body. Despite her fragility, her face glowed and her eyes sparkled as if she had just woken from a long and restful sleep.

'My word, they are just beautiful!' she smiled coyly when I handed her the flowers, 'Mel, aren't they glorious?' her smile broadened as she looked up at him.

No matter how hard he tried to hide it, Mel's face depicted his obvious concern for Martha so it took me by surprise when he suddenly put his arms around me and gave me a huge hug.

'Wow, I must bring flowers more often!' I laughed as I hugged back.

'That's from both of us…it was lovely to join in the fun last night!' Mel smiled warmly.

'Well it wouldn't have been as successful if you hadn't been there so it's me who should be thanking you. I'm just so sorry we tired you out Martha.'

'Now, Cassie please don't make me cross with that nonsense! Mel darling would you put these blooms in a vase for me, there is one in the cupboard by the sink…and maybe we could tempt Cassie to stay a while if you pop the kettle on?'

Mel's expression stopped me from protesting any more, so I pulled a chair up next to the sofa.

76

'There now,' Martha sighed triumphantly, 'come and tell me if I missed out on any thing after I left last night!'

We drank tea and chatted for a while about how well every one had got along at the party but I felt there was an obvious avoidance of discussing Martha's health. I had hoped that they would feel they could confide in me but I realised that maybe it was still too soon for that. I reached over to take Martha's hand and felt reassured by the warmth I felt when she reciprocated with a gentle squeeze; I looked into her face searching for answers but saw only a quiet strength and determination. The evening light was fading as Mel began to switch on the variety of table and standard lamps scattered about the room, then just as I stood to take my leave I heard a key in the lock accompanied by a knock on the door. The knowing smile that passed between my two friends confirmed who it was before I even heard Tom call out, 'Is anyone home? Or have you two revellers gone out on the town again, two nights in a row is it?'

I was still processing the fact that Tom had his own key, when he entered the room carrying what appeared to be a whole month's groceries.

'Hey Cassie' he winked at me as though he had expected to see me there; then turning to Martha, 'and how's the party girl doing, you're looking a tad more rested.' Tom quickly took over where I had left off, sitting by her side and holding her hand all the while chatting gently to us all. 'I picked up some bits so that you guys didn't need to worry for a few days but if there's anything else you need in the mean time just give me a buzz ok?'

I couldn't quite understand what I was feeling but I was pretty sure it had a depth to it that I was going to have to seriously analyse once my brain was more focused. I helped Mel put away the groceries letting him direct me to where everything was kept, all the while I could hear Tom in discussion with Martha, and though I couldn't quite make out the conversation, it was clear that he was lifting her spirits and soon her girlish laughter reached the kitchen and I could see the weight physically lift from Mel's shoulders.

With Mel's permission I jotted my mobile number down and pinned it onto the notice board in the kitchen, 'Promise me you'll call me if you need anything…I mean it's not as if I have far to come is it?' I smiled giving him a hug.

Martha cupped my face in her hands as I leaned over to kiss her cheek. 'Thank you angel, now please no silly worrying, I will be just fine. Come by in a couple of days and we will have a stroll along the front. The summer will be here and gone before you know it and when you start work in September we won't get to see so much of you.'

'You must be joking, I'm going to need to come and tell you about all the mistakes I am bound to make as a rookie!'

'You should have more faith in yourself young lady and any way you don't need any excuse to come and visit with us!' Mel chimed in.

With the mood lifted, Tom saw me to the door. 'I'm going to stay a while longer, just to see them settled for the evening like. It means a lot to them Cassie…that you care, you know? Thanks darlin.' Then as if it was the most natural thing to do he planted a kiss on my forehead.

Back in my flat, I spent a lot of time pacing up and down and smiling to myself. I kept touching my forehead like some love sick teenager, worried that the warmth I still felt there would disappear. Christ, it was only a peck on the forehead after all, as way of a thank you for being there. I poured myself a glass of wine and opened up the balcony doors, the air was fresh and there was a slight breeze, 'you do realise the sun won't always shine in Brighton don't you?' Lucy's words came to me while I sat looking out into the night with a blanket around my shoulders. I felt very confused all of a sudden. My life had changed for the better in so many ways but something was nagging at me telling me not to let my guard down and get complacent, urging me to be prepared for things to keep on changing. I was starting to depend on Sanctuary House to give me the answers to everything, why would I ever think a building could hold that much power? Then before I could answer my own questions there was a deep rumble of thunder followed by a flash of lightening that lit the whole sky up silhouetting the skeleton of the old pier in all its crumbling glory. I was sure I felt the foundations of the house shift along with my mood once again.

There would be no running away this time, I'd have to face my new life head on with all its challenges; no one said it would be a walk on the beach but this part of the journey would be different, this time I didn't feel alone.

***

[19]

On Monday morning I took delivery of my official job acceptance letter along with a slightly daunting wedge of paperwork including detailed terms and conditions the likes of which I hadn't seen for quite some time. After an initial wobble, I skimmed through and was reminded how these documents were always very wordy but I reassured myself that at least I had the luxury of being able to read through them at my leisure in order to absorb all the essential bits of information. I felt a renewed sense of purpose and decided it was as good a time as any to start preparing myself for this exciting career change. Through out my working life, I had always accepted any job as a means to an end, always making sure I was home for Ben. There was a time when I held down three jobs; office cleaning in the morning, shop-work in the middle of the day and onto another cleaning job before rushing home to make dinner. As Ben got older, I was able to be a bit more selective but it was always about survival, job satisfaction didn't really come into it. My last place of employment had been as a front of house receptionist at a local theatre, and although only a small venue they had been very strict on dress code and the uniform consisted of white fitted blouse, black skirt or trousers, black tailored jacket and black shoes. No individuality and incredibly uncomfortable. So naturally, whilst scanning through my new job description, I headed for the most important paragraph in the t's and c's and was delighted to find a fairly casual approach to work wear. This was not just about physical comfort but it also meant that I didn't have to assert any impression of authority.

After my third wardrobe check, I took a look at my finances and thought that although I was going to have to be a bit more frugal, I could at least treat myself to a couple of new items of clothing. I'd existed on porridge before now, besides I was in need of a confidence boost.

'Believe in your self Cassie'-someone had said that to me once, but for the life of me I couldn't recall who. Pep talk done

I was finally ready to hit the shops of Brighton town. It felt good to be ticking another thing off my 'to do' list and I was gradually allowing myself to realise I did have the potential to start my new life.

I spent a couple of hours wandering around the shopping centre before finally heading back to the hub of the Lanes where I managed to find everything I needed without breaking the bank. Heading home I decided I would not be tempted to wander past Tom's studio but instead I took the high road straight back to the house. Back in my flat, I bit the bullet and called Professor Bennett's' secretary to arrange a visit. Once again, my call was greeted with friendly enthusiasm and I was immediately put at ease when she said,

'You are welcome to call in at any time Cassie, but if you would like to phone in on the day, we can arrange for someone to be here to meet you.'

Just as I was going through my diary and smugly congratulating myself on everything I had achieved that day there was a knock at the door, I was starting to recognise that a knock could only mean a neighbour so my stomach gave its customary flip and my smile was emerging before I even opened the door to Tom.

'Oh hi' I said way too casually.

'Pub crawl?'

'Who?'

'We' said Tom pointing from me to him.

It took a moment before I realised he was waiting for a response.

'Uhm-Ok, when?'

'Fifteen minutes?'

I glanced at my wrist to look at a non existent watch and noticing his smile, I shrugged, 'Force of habit!'

'It's just gone five thirty,' he held up his equally bare wrist,' I figure by the time we head out it will be considered respectable!'

'Hah! How very gallant. Would you like to come in while I just grab my bag and freshen up?'

'Nah you're grand, I need to do the same so I'll see you down by the front door.'

'What you need to grab your bag?'

'Would that be a problem like?'

Those Irish eyes were smiling.

'See you in a bit Tom.'

I was aware that as I stepped back into my flat there was already an internal dialogue going on.

Firstly, 'What just happened?'

Secondly, 'Don't go over thinking this Cassie.'

Thirdly, 'As lovely as he seems I don't really know the guy.'

Finally, 'Fifteen minutes isn't long and I've already spent two of those rooted to the spot.

A plan of action ensued which involved the face, teeth, shake and spray method.

Freshen face with a splash of cold water. Brush teeth making breath minty fresh (even though it was about to be sullied by the intake of alcohol) and ensure no left over greenery from lunch time sandwich. Throw head forward and shake hair, I have no idea if this helps the appearance as it always leaves me too dizzy to look in the mirror, but my locks are way to unruly for a brush. Finally, spray the air with not too expensive cologne and do a slow-mo walk through its falling vapours. I learnt this trick whilst working at the theatre, from an actress who was touring in a play entitled—AS YOU THOUGHT YOU LIKED IT. The play was an almighty flop but the actress will have a place in my toilette forever.

Next; check bag for phone, money and keys – eleven minutes, just three minutes left to text Lucy. The golden rule, always let each other know where you're at if safety is a concern. This seemed a bit ridiculous when I thought of Tom but she would never forgive me.

HEY LUCE, INVITED ON A PUB CRAWL BY TOM. JUST ABOUT TO LEAVE BUT WILL TEXT ASAP AND CHAT LATER. LOVEYA CASS XX

So, feeling a little flushed from my mission barely possible antics, I gave a quick glance around the flat and headed out the door. I refrained from skipping down the stairs as I didn't want a repeat of the gallery incident which had left me with just the one strong ankle and very little dignity. Plus I was forty five years old.

Good as his word Tom was waiting by the front door looking calm and totally unflustered.

'Hi. I wonder should I just pop in and let M&M know we're heading out?'

'No need, I already had a wee chat.'

Now when had he had time to do that? I mean granted, I can't see him going through the face, teeth, shake and spray routine but still, he seemed to have covered a lot of bases for our casual pub crawl.

We stepped out into a lovely balmy, coastal breeze. I glanced over at Tom and patted my bag, 'Did you forget something?'

'Ah sure no, I figured I'd go with minimal accessories this evening.'

'Apparently, there is one pub for every 250 residents in Brighton, so what's your strategy Tom?'

'Now did I say we could finish the crawl in one night? But let's start with one of my favourite local bars'

***

As it happened we didn't crawl very far to that pub, it being a short walk from the beach and in the heart of The Lanes. We arrived early enough to secure a nice spot in the small but pretty beer garden, although I don't think we would have had a problem as it quickly became obvious that Tom was known. As he ordered our drinks I couldn't decide if this was because he was a regular patron or a local artist, when I commented on this I managed to refrain from using the obvious play on words.

'Ah well, yes I do like the place. It dates back to the sixteenth century, so plenty of history in these walls upon which they have been known to display my work from time to time. What do you think of it?'

'I like it very much. It has a good feel to the building and I'm sure Ray and Andy would appreciate the colourful display of hanging baskets and troughs!'

'Aye, well I think they may have had a little say in that!'

'Really? Blimey I've got some catching up to do with my neighbours!'

There was a brief lull where I did that self conscious peering into my drink thing.

'Cassie, I need to talk to you about Martha.'

My head snapped up and I was no longer concerned with looking directly into Toms' eyes, 'What about Martha?'

'No, no, she's fine right now. It's just that they, Mel and Martha, asked if could have a chat with you.'

So asking me out had been a bit of a smokescreen for him to complete some allotted task. Tom didn't even look uncomfortable; on the contrary, there was a look of relief on his face as he took another mouthful from his pint.

I was struggling to know what I was feeling. I think betrayed and slightly embarrassed might describe the reason I could feel a flush rise to my cheeks and the sting of tears to my eyes.

'You know Tom; you didn't need to go to all this trouble. You could have just said what you needed to on my doorstep.

'Jaisus Cassie! It's not like that at all!'

At that moment the bartender appeared with more drinks, which I didn't remember ordering. I was glaring at Tom now.

'Sorry, I took the liberty of getting another round, in case....'

'Oh what? In case I needed something to keep me here?'

Tom looked genuinely hurt and a little bemused by what I realised was a pretty childish reaction. There came a distraction from my phone with an incoming message from Lucy.

HOPE YOU'RE HAVING A GRAND TIME! ENJOY (DARLIN')! HUGS LUCE XX

I felt a lump rise to my throat as I sent a quick smiley face emoji in reply so that she wouldn't worry. I was trembling as I returned the phone to my bag.

'Listen, Cassie will you at least have this drink with me while I explain? I probably didn't handle this so well, but you need to know that I actually told Mel and Martha that I was thinking of asking you out tonight. Mel thought I was punching above my weight like, Martha on the other hand was delighted.'

How did he do that? Melt my insides before I had even finished being angry with him?

So it was, that the pub crawl came to a halt while I listened to Tom's explanation, it transpired that M&M had felt that it was time for me to know the full extent of Martha's illness but they were concerned that I would find it too upsetting hearing it first hand. So, when Tom revealed his plan to ask me out for a drink they asked if he wouldn't mind sharing a few details.

Martha had been diagnosed with a low-grade follicular Lymphoma when she was just 63years old. It's a disease which goes into remission but as time advances the relapses become more regular. Martha was now 78 years old.

I didn't know how to react to this information without knowing more,

'Oh Tom...all that time. What a brave and beautiful lady; and Melvin bless his heart that explains why he doesn't let her out of his sight. Does she need to undergo any specific treatment?'

'It's pretty much watch and wait. So she has blood tests every 6 months but I think they may become more frequent and they will adjust her medications accordingly.'

'Do you think now that I know they will be ok sharing a bit more with me?'

'I'm betting they'd share their life story with you! They wouldn't have wanted you to know otherwise. Maybe, concentrate more on their amazing past journey rather than what's to come though eh darlin'? They have taken you into their hearts Cass, there's no bigger compliment than that.'

I raised my glass saying, 'To our dearest M&M and their continuing journey!'

'I'll second that!'

Once I had convinced Tom I was ok, and that the reason I needed to use the cloakroom was due to the fact that I had consumed two pints of Guinness in quick succession, I quickly messaged Lucy:

ALL OK. TOO MUCH TO TEXT BUT WILL CHAT SOON, PROMISE! CX

A speedy response made me imagine Lucy glued to the phone waiting for my messages.

LET ME KNOW YOURE HOME SAFE. WE CAN CHAT TOMORROW. LX

When I returned to the table Tom was settling the bill. I was really hoping our friendship was still intact so I offered to buy the next round at the second pub.

I was waiting with baited breath for the reason he would give to end the evening early.

'Have you eaten?'

I was not expecting that.

'Actually no, I just realised I haven't, probably not wise to continue.'

'Well, I was wondering if you fancied walking back up the boardwalk and grabbing some grub at my place?'

'What at the gallery?'

He let out a hearty laugh, 'Well not unless you want a sandwich! Eejit!

No I was thinking more of cooking up my famous pasta back at the flat if you think you're brave enough!'

'That sounds great I'm starving! I can grab a bottle of wine from my place on the way up.'

It was lovely strolling back along the boardwalk and we fell into a relaxed conversation about cooking and our favourite go to dishes. I felt it was only fair to warn him of my vegetarian status.

'To be honest, although I've been known to eat chicken from time to time, I'm pretty much veggie myself. However, I'm from dairy farming stock so nothing could persuade me to go vegan!'

'Oh, I tried that once but I couldn't get on with the non dairy cheeses.' I wrinkled up my nose and he smiled in response. We had reached the steps up to the pavement in what seemed no time at all.

'Now, knowing your relationship with steps, will you be going first so I can be there to catch you, or would you like me to go ahead and lend you a hand?'

'Oy! Don't get too lippy matey! You go first, age before beauty and all that.'

As we entered the house we both instinctively tilted our heads towards Martha and Melvin's door.

'Don't worry Cass, there's nothing wrong with their hearing, they'll know we're home safe.'

I nodded, acknowledging how well he knew our neighbours. I did a quick detour into my flat to pick up a bottle of wine then followed Tom up the stairway. He had left his door slightly ajar so I knocked gently before stepping into a space that I had not been expecting.

'Woah!' I gasped; because although there was still a little natural light coming from outside it was as though I had entered into a vast area of illumination. I hadn't given much thought as to what Tom's flat would be like. I think having seen everyone's space within the house, I had forgotten the positioning and the necessity for the design I was now seeing. It was spectacular. Open plan was too loose a term for it. It ran the whole length of the roof space in the house and what I was seeing now was an area that was obviously a studio. There were a couple of soft sofas, and small driftwood coffee tables scattered along the left hand side but the eye was drawn to the working area where paint splattered dust sheets had been pushed aside towards an assortment of easels displaying various works in progress. Nestled alongside were trestle tables that held all the tools of Tom's trade. The colour that all this added to the room seemed almost contrived. The brightness was achieved by various huge dormer windows either side of the exposed rafters and everything from the floorboards upwards was painted white. At the end of this glorious runway was a galley kitchen and breakfast bar, behind which Tom was already busy collecting together items for dinner from the cupboards.

'Is it too much?' he broke into my reverie. I must have appeared mesmerised.

'It's very different, in a beautiful way; just a bit hard to get my head around at the moment!'

'The space carries on behind the kitchen here and things might be a bit more familiar to you there, go and check it out while I make a start on grub. Make use of anything you like.' I put the bottle of wine on the counter and went in search of the bathroom.

I felt a bit like Alice in Wonderland as the space narrowed and the floor curved slightly to the left. I past a door that was closed, then a little further on was another door that led into the

87

bathroom. What really threw me was the balcony at the very end of the corridor which provided yet more natural light. I had always assumed it would be directly above my own but it was in fact, curved around the end corner of the building in a semi circle. My first thought was that the doors must have been a bugger to shape; quickly followed by, how did I not notice all this! I made a promise to myself to study the exterior of the house in more detail. I quickly used the bathroom and couldn't resist peeking behind the closed door.

I felt a bit voyeuristic looking into Tom's bedroom but it was quite similar in size to my own with minimal but tasteful furniture and tidier than I expected. I realised that he only had one bedroom which would account for the massive floor space in the main room.

'Can I give you a hand Tom?'

'Nothing to do here, it's real basic. Maybe set the counter and open the wine?'

Tom's basic pasta was delicious and really welcome. We chatted about anything and everything, dipping in and out of each others history.

I learnt that Thomas Moynihan was the fifth child amongst eight.

The Moynihan family owned quite a substantial dairy farm. Home was the small town of Clonakilty; it lay at the head of the tidal Clonakilty Bay which, being surrounded by green hills and pasture, lent itself well to dairy cattle.

When I declared my admiration for his mother giving birth to eight children he joked about the expense of farm labour.

'It sounds beautiful Tom, you must miss it.'

'I miss it well enough to make visits regularly but there isn't enough holding me there. I think being the fifth child maybe I felt the need to express myself in other ways. Don't get me wrong now, there's an abundance of love in my family, but we're all individuals choosing our own paths in the world and just knowing we are all there for each other is the grounding you know? How about you Cassie? What brought you here?'

'Christ Tom, that's a loaded question that I might need to answer another time. Sometimes, I wish I had someone to watch over me, someone who knows me better than I know myself.

I've not had the luxury of family back up such as your self but hey every one's situation is different.' Tom was looking at me as if he wanted to know more; but I wasn't ready for that.

'The food was perfect Tom, now how about I wash the dishes?'

'Why would you want to be doing that now?'

'What, you've not heard the public announcement? Only use your dishwasher when full!'

'Haha, you crack me up girl!'

We fell back into small talk and friendly banter while we shared the clearing up. It felt good and weirdly familiar, as if I had known this man forever. There were a million questions going around in my head but I thought maybe it was a good time to bring the evening to a close.

'I should be heading back'

'It being a long journey 'n all?'

He was smiling but I was quite touched that he sounded a little disappointed.

'No, really Tom, it's been lovely but it's getting late and I need my beauty sleep!

'In that case I'll walk you home'

Standing outside my door I was so tempted to ask him in for a last drink.

'Well thank you kind sir'.

'To be continued?'

There was the briefest of pauses.

'I'd like that a lot' I smiled.

'Grand. Oh and Cassie, you don't need it you know.'

'What?'

'Your beauty sleep... you don't need it.'

He briefly took my hand and gave it a gentle squeeze before starting up the stairs,

'I'll be in touch Cass.'

This melting feeling was becoming a regular occurrence.

[20]

I woke early on Tuesday morning after a fitful sleep. Stepping out onto the balcony the air was fresh and welcoming, so I wrapped a woolen shawl around my shoulders and cradled a cup of hot water and lemon. This was my morning 'go to' beverage when I needed to clear my head of detritus, self inflicted or otherwise.

I was desperately trying to recall all the events of the previous day but I was struggling to get beyond the memory of Tom saying, 'I'll be in touch Cass'.

I pulled myself up sharp and decided to quickly shower and drag my bicycle from the shed for its maiden voyage along the cycle path towards Hove. It was far too early to call Lucy so I charged my phone with the intention of contacting her when I stopped for a break. I crept down the stairs and along the hallway to collect my bike from the garden shed. I had forgotten it was a weekday and that 7.30 a.m. wasn't regarded as early for most hard working people but I was still surprised to find Andy and Ray already having coffee in the garden.

'Hey Cassie, you're an early bird today!' Andy greeted me.

'Come and join us, I can grab another cup' Ray suggested.

'No, please sit, I already had one. I'm so sorry to disturb you; I'll need to get used to early starts soon enough so I thought I'd bring my bike out of retirement and wake myself up!'

Having extracted my transport from the shed and apologised to the garden spider for dismantling her home from the wheel spokes, I wasn't surprised to find the tyres were looking a bit squishy. I proceeded to inflate them while Andy and Ray looked on.

'I wasn't expecting a warm up exercise at the start of my ride!' I puffed.

The boys glanced at each other and chuckled.

'What?' I felt an innuendo coming on, 'Well lovely, if you will have secret liaisons you have to expect your energy levels to be a bit low.'

I felt my cheeks flush and not from the effort of using the bicycle pump. Glancing up I saw Mel at his kitchen window, waving and sending me a cheeky smile. I blew a kiss his way and then flopped on a chair next to the boys.

'No secrets here then?'

'I'm afraid not sweetie and if we didn't have to head off we would be interrogating you further, isn't that right Ray?'

Ray was nodding in agreement whilst gathering up the coffee cups. They were clearly enjoying my embarrassment.

I threw my hands up, 'Honestly, guys there's nothing to tell! Don't worry about the door; I'll lock it on my way out.'

'You have a great ride Cassie, we'll catch up later!' they were still giggling and jostling for the door like two kids.

'Awh come on, really?' I protested as I watched them disappear into the house.

As soon as I was sure the coast was clear, I grabbed my bike and made a quick exit; thankfully I made it out to the cycle path without any further encounters.

The benefit of the coastline cycle path, aside from the obvious, was the safety of being separated from heavy traffic. Of course, you still have to be aware of other cyclists, roller-bladers, skate-boarders and of course dogs and their humans but all of that was so much more stimulating than being stuck amongst the more aggressive and oppressive drone of motorised transport.

On the whole, and especially early in the day, bathing in the briny air was a peaceful and salutiferous experience and by the time I'd reached Hove, my skin was tingling and my whole being buzzed with life. There was another buzzing coming from my back pack, 'That'll be Lucy' I smiled. So I headed to the boating lake café for breakfast, taking off my helmet and jacket I let the warmth of the morning sun ease its way through to my bones. The café was just preparing to open so I took a seat by the lake to check my phone. Two messages; one from Lucy telling me she was home till lunch time if I fancied a chat and the other was an unknown number;

HEY CASS, I HOPE YOU DON'T MIND THAT I STOLE YOUR CONTACT FROM M&M...IM NOT SURE WHY WE DIDN'T SWAP NUMBERS BEFORE? ANYWAYS, JUST

TO LET YOU KNOW I'M OFF HOME TO IRELAND THIS MORNING. I DID KNOCK YOUR DOOR BUT MY INFORMANTS TELL ME YOU SNUCK OUT FOR A BIKE RIDE EARLY ON. IM GLAD MY COOKING HASN'T LAID YOU LOW! I SHOULD ONLY BE GONE A COUPLE OF DAYS THIS TIME, BUT I WAS SERIOUS ABOUT CONTINUING THE PUB CRAWL SOMETIME IF YOUR UP FOR IT? YOU HAVE MY NUMBER NOW SO. TOM X

I read the message twice just to be sure. Then I called Lucy and in her defence she remained patient and remarkably silent all the way through my portrayal of the last 24 hours.

'So, I'm guessing the ball's in my court,' I sipped my coffee and took a chunk out of a chewy flapjack whilst I waited for the barrage of questions.

'Luce? You still there?'

'Yep'

'You've gone awful quiet.'

'Hmmm, just thinking. So, apart from the slightly rocky start, you two appear to have had a great evening in each others company?'

'Just lovely.' I smiled.

'Then Tom invited you home and cooked you dinner?'

'Yep, and very nice it was too!'

'He then proceeded to escort you up a whole flight of stairs to your door, where he paid you a very sweet compliment, although I feel the man may have still had his beer goggles on!'

'Jeez Lucy, what's with the inquisition!'

'Well, I was just wondering why you are spending your time talking to me instead of replying to Ireland's version of Mr Darcy!'

It was something I needed to work on; making decisions that weren't loaded with self doubt. I thought I had made a lot of progress since moving to Brighton, but Lucy was right of course, it was time to take another leap into the unknown and be a bit more adventurous. After all, reassurance from others means nothing if you don't believe in yourself. Back at Sanctuary House, I locked my bike away and sat in the garden for a moment to compose a reply to Tom. There was a lot I wanted to say and questions to ask but maybe that's what

92

second dates were for, so in the end I went for simplistic honesty.

HI TOM... OF COURSE I DON'T MINDYOU TAKING MY NUMBER, ALTHOUGH, IM PRETTY SURE M&M WOULDN'T LET YOU GET AWAY WITH THEFT, SO I CAN ONLY ASSUME YOU ARE ALL IN THIS TOGETHER!

I HOPE YOUR TRIP HOME GOES WELL, LET ME KNOW WHEN YOU'RE BACK SO WE CAN SORT OUR NEXT BOOZY STUMBLE! MY TURN TO COOK- IF YOU'RE MAN ENOUGH? SEE YOU SOON. CASS XX

I hesitated briefly, and then quickly pressed send before I could change my mind, particularly about the two kisses. The speed of his reply took me by surprise.

'MAN ENOUGH? IS THIS STILL ABOUT THE HANDBAG? TO BE DISCUSSED. TOM X

I resisted carrying on the conversation like a giddy teenager and just sent a thumbs up emoji, then quickly put my phone away. Looking up I saw M&M at their kitchen door, beckoning me to go in and join them.

[21]

It always amazes me how some people are always ready for visitors. If guests arrive at my door unexpectedly they are lucky if they get milk in their tea let alone anything to eat with it. M&M seemed to be able to magic up pots of tea before you even stepped over the threshold; and proper tea in a teapot, not your lazy t-bag chucked in a mug affair. Melvin and Martha evoked a very distant memory of my grandmother, I think on my father's side. On our rare visits, the tea table would groan with home baked cakes all set out on delicate china plates covered with lace doilies. Also on offer were immaculate triangle sandwiches with all the crusts missing, it was a while before I realised that this was a deliberate act of bread butchery and was considered the height of afternoon tea etiquette, possibly a throw back from the Victorian era.

I just remember fearing that with every chime of the grandfather clock, I might flinch and drop something on the immaculate carpet.

M&M also, always had a full table and a never ending teapot but the difference being that the welcome was warm and never contrived, and as perfect as their home was, no one could ever feel uncomfortable in their company.

Moments later I was sat in the comfort of the sitting room clutching my cheese sandwich, substantial and thankfully still retaining its crusts. After discussing my morning trip to Hove and the many alternative scenic routes I would be able to explore, I decided to address the proverbial elephant in the room.

'My goodness, you two are visibly bursting! As I have discovered nothing is sacred here, but let me put your minds at rest. Tom and I had a great evening and yes there will be a second date.'

They were still perched on the edge of their chairs as if waiting for some further revelation. Martha seemed barely able to stop from clapping her hands in glee.

'I promise, I will keep you informed. Although, I'm sure Tom is more than capable of that; given how close you guys are.'

I hoped that this hinted at the fact that they had been very much a part of our conversation during our evening out, and that I was now more aware of Martha's situation.

Relaxing into the plush sofa I sighed, 'I am really going to have to stop filling myself with all your delicious grub; I will never fit into my new work clothes!'

Martha reached for my hand, 'Oh, Cassie we haven't had time to congratulate you properly on your new job, you must be thrilled!'

'Ah thank you, yes I'm a bit nervous but excited about a new challenge. More importantly I am just so relieved that I get to stay here!'

'Well, that was never in any doubt dear.'

'Ha, well I think the landlord would have had something to say about squatting rights and besides, although I'm a free spirit, that's not quite my style'

M&M have a way of conveying there is something to tell without even speaking.

'What?'

'Well, it just so happens that we know the landlord well and we're pretty sure he would have allowed you to stay, no question. Isn't that so Martha?'

The penny always takes a while to drop with me but for some reason, this time I knew before it even reached its destination.

'Tom?' I said slowly shaking my head.

'Yes dear, Tom. Mel, could you get Cassie a drop of something stronger while we continue our chatter.'

Over the course of the next couple of hours I learnt so much more about the history of Sanctuary House and its inhabitants but rather than it coming as a surprise it felt more like a gradual awareness as the jigsaw puzzle came together.

Martha and Melvin were both wartime children but from very different back grounds so for them to have found each other in the post war wilderness was a story in itself.

Martha had been born in Springfield, Massachusetts in 1935. Joe and Nancy Carter were loving parents who envisaged a happy future with a growing family but just as they began to plan for a second child, World War Two broke out, changing everybody's lives forever. Joe joined the US Air Force and as soon as Martha was old enough to go to school, Nancy began working in a munitions factory.

One of the highlights of Martha's week would be when her mother picked her up from school and announced they were going to the movies; this happened at least once a week, depending on what was showing .There was quite a wide variety, from Casablanca to Disney's Draftee Duck; but Martha soon developed a passion for musicals and she lost count of the amount of times she begged her mother to sit through Yankee Doodle Dandy, Ship Ahoy or Me and My Gal. Once home she would try to replicate each and every dance step until she was able to put on a full show for family and friends in their little back yard, always dreaming of making it to Broadway. One of her mother's friends knew the owner of the local dance school and she suggested that Nancy enrolled Martha for classes, so although going to the movies was still a regular outing; dancing soon became a real consuming passion, much to Nancy's relief.

It never occurred to Martha that her father would never witness how his little girl had grown into a confident performer but tragically his plane was brought down over Germany in 1944.

As war was coming to a close in1945, Martha at 10 years old had not only lost her father but began to feel increasingly distanced from her mother. They lived alongside each other but Nancy had lost all interest in pretty much everything, including Martha and her progress at the dance school. When Martha reached fifteen the school put her forward for a scholarship to go to a New York dance and drama boarding Academy. When she announced this to her mother, she had expected the news to be greeted with some resistance but instead it was as if her mother was relieved,

'Well that's great honey, you'll make your own way now, and it's what your daddy would have wanted.'

Martha didn't allow herself to process this response and instead focused on preparing to leave home at 16 years of age.

'Not long after I left for New York, my mother wrote to tell me she was to remarry. After that I'm afraid our relationship became more strained and although I would still go home and spend time with her, I found I just could not connect with her new husband. Communication between my mother and I became increasingly difficult. Once I started moving around the country; I wrote to her often and even sent tickets for some of the off Broadway shows I was in; she never came and rarely replied. It makes me very sad that she didn't get to meet my Mel or at least to see how happy I was; because although it was daddy who had the love of music, it was mom taking me to the movies that ignited my passion for dance. When she got sick I managed to spend a little time with her, but she barely recognised me towards the end and strangely I didn't recognise her either. I think the tears I shed at her funeral were more for how different things could have been and not really for her passing.'

I had been transfixed while Martha relayed her story and so was unaware that Mel had sat alongside her holding her hand.

'Martha, that's an incredible story! Following your passion when you were so young and alone must have been really tough. Thank you so much for sharing that with me; but please, you mustn't over tire your self.'

'Yes well that's only half the tale my dear. So if you can bear to hear more, perhaps you would join us for dinner later?'

'Listen, why don't I leave you two in peace a while and we can meet for breakfast in the morning instead?'

'I think that's a great idea Cassie, that way my lady can strengthen her vocal chords!'

Mel was chuckling but I could sense he was relieved at my suggestion.

I was pretty exhausted myself, so took myself up the stairs to try and unravel my thoughts before sleep.

Martha's story weighed heavily in my heart all evening. I just could not conceive how a young child was able to survive such trauma. I wept when I thought of her courage and how

97

even now, in her twilight years, she was still having to draw on that extraordinary strength.

It was passed midnight when I messaged Ben to ask if there was any chance of a catch up the following day. I really missed someone to share my thoughts with, but I instantly regretted sending such a late message. Of course, instead of just leaving it, I then sent another message to apologise for sending the first one. I went to bed wondering if I should ring him early the next day to apologise for both messages in case they had disturbed him. With a feeling of despair at my own indecisiveness, I drifted in and out of sleep.

[22]

I awoke at 5.00 am with a head full of so many questions for too many people; it was painfully akin to a bad hangover with none of the pleasure involved. I chucked on some clothes and crept down to the sea front. It was silent and beautiful, the sky was just unwrapping its early morning light and it reminded me of one of Tom's paintings; I suddenly wished he was there to help me work through my thoughts. While I stood listening to the gentle hushing of the waves against shingle, I tried to visualise my mind being cleansed in the same way. Instead, I felt lost and alone for the first time in a while; but being realistic I knew I shouldn't expect too much considering my track record.

The morning air was a little too fresh so I headed back for a warm shower and some pain relief to try and clear my head.

Part of me was eager to hear more of M&M's story but I was also aware of how draining it must be to relive their past. I prepared a large bowl of summer fruits, grabbed a tub of yoghurt and made my way down to their flat.

Mel opened the door and greeted me with his usual warm smile.

'Well good morning Cassie, I see you're spoiling us today!'

Spotting Martha behind him I was pleased to see she looked more rested.

'Good morning to you both! I wasn't sure what to contribute but hopefully this is ok for now.'

Once we had settled around the table I felt a little easier and thought perhaps tiredness was the reason for the strange mood that had descended on me the previous evening.

'I have to tell you both how privileged I feel that you have chosen to share your remarkable story with me, although I've no idea why you would choose to do so.'

'Well now Cassie, it just feels the right thing to do. Our story is not so unique and it is certainly no secret; but it belongs to us and sometimes you need to know the history to make sense of the present.'

Melvin Malkiovich was born Malik Malkovich. The subtle change of name came about more through an administrative error rather than any attempt at anonymity.

Melvin was born in Poland in 1930 making him 5 years older than Martha. His mother Zofia Kowalski was Polish, while his father, also Malik, had left his home in Ukraine to find work and he began by helping Zofia's family on their small farm.

Melvyn explained that it was with great regret that he knew very little about his parent's history but he remembered his father joking that he had come to Poland to work the beautiful land and had landed himself a beautiful wife.

'What I do know is that we had very little but wanted for nothing. As an only child, I was given the best start in life that my parents could provide.'

The small parcel of land left to them by Zofia's parents was mainly arable with a few chickens and milking goats. Mel had enjoyed having free rein of the farm and even helped out with some of the simpler tasks but it was always Malik and Zofias wish for their son to experience greater things in life. They encouraged him with his school studies and in an attempt to curb his love of the outdoors he was sent to his Uncle Yosup in Ukraine during school holidays. Yosyp was himself a teacher and with no family of his own at that time, he adored spending the vacations with his nephew.

'Uncle Yosyp was so very different from Poppa. Academic and full of fire and ideas! He cared for me and encouraged me in ways his older brother could not. Not only that but he was somehow in possession of a beautiful Bechstein piano! I knew not to ask how. No matter, I fell in love for the first time when I was introduced to that amazing instrument. The second and last time? Well!' with a shrug of his shoulders Melvin smiled at Martha.

'There you have it Cassie dear; I was never to be his first love!'

'But, between my parents, and Uncle Yosyp, oy vey, what a joyous start to my young life!'

Mel recalled being told by his parents that he was to extend his school holidays with Uncle Yosyp in the August of 1939.

'I learnt later of course that they must have known Poland was about to be occupied by both the Nazis and the Soviet Union. They were trying to protect me, to give me a chance and that was the last time...'

I reached over to take his hand, 'Mel please don't...'

'No, bubala, altz iz gut...to shed a tear or two after so many years is a great sign of love and respect'

I was choked, not only by his great wisdom but I had never heard Mel speak Yiddish before and it gave a more personal insight into his past.

The last Mel had heard of his parents was that they had been taken to Treblinka prisoner of war camp in Germany.

The situation in Ukraine was by no means safe but Yosyp managed to keep them together, living secret lives and surviving in and around the forests; relying on the kindness of friends and connections. Eventually by 1945 they emerged from their almost feral existence and were placed in a US zone German displaced persons camp.

'At such a young age I knew not to ask why or how, but I was convinced my Uncle Yosyp had a grander plan,' Mel shrugged, 'conversations were had and documents were obtained and eventually after some years of negotiating we were able to migrate to the US. Our visas stated Yosyps' profession as teacher and mine as Student of Music. I think the fact that Yosyp declared him self as my only remaining blood relative and therefore technically he would be responsible for my well being, helped our application. If I asked about my parents, my uncle would only hang his head and say, Malik boychik, they are no more. After a while, I stopped asking, but I think he knew more than he was willing to share.'

Mel and his Uncle Yosyp settled in a Polish community, Polonia, in Chicago Illinois. They began by taking on manual labour but both made sure they pursued their individual crafts. Yosyp teaching in the evenings and weekends while Mel worked his way around the bars and theatres, playing piano and tending bar.

'Uncle Yosyp met and married Agata and by the time they started their family I was already making plans to try my luck in New York, which of course is how I met meyn lib!'

Martha looked to me with a gentle smile, 'My love' she translated.

I was astounded. 'You had lived so many lives by that time!'

'Yes, many journeys and hardships but we are fortunate to have travelled this last part of our journey together.'

The morning was all but gone when I suggested that perhaps we could sit in the garden for some air, 'Unless you have had enough of me?'

'No, I think tea in the garden is just what we all need!

There was a final piece to the jigsaw but I wasn't sure if now was the time.

However, I think M&M were keen to move on to the happiness they had found together so they explained that after a lifetime of treading the boards all over the world they were drawn to Europe and more specifically to the UK.

'We had many happy times here and had made so many friends along the way that we felt we should aim to settle here before we got too old! We didn't want to just give it all up, but it was my wonderful Mel who suggested we try to open a Dance and Drama academy for less fortunate children.'

So, it turned out that whilst on a visit to friends in 1965, they stumbled upon Sanctuary House; they ploughed everything they had saved into the project and fought for charity funding. The ground floor was accommodation whilst the remainder of the building was converted to studio space.

'Oh but Cassie the building lived up to its name many times over; the children and young adults who have been through these doors have gone on to do wonderful things with their lives and not just in the arts. The most important thing we gave them was pride in themselves and courage to be any one they wanted to be!'

Mel and Martha were beaming by the end of their story.

'So, what happened next? I asked

'Ah, well we think that maybe Tom can take it from here as really that is his part of the story.'

'Ah, so I guess the second date is essential'

'Well, we kind of hoped that would be the case.'

'You two are such matchmakers and I would hate to disappoint you.' I smiled.

I thanked them again for sharing their incredible stories, and hugging them both, I promised to look in on them soon. I left them sitting in the garden, holding hands engrossed in personal conversation; looking back at them, they looked for all the world like a beautiful sculpture, their heads close, rapt in their love for each other, two sides of a puzzle that were a perfect fit.

[23]

Ben didn't call; and I didn't message him to ask why. Possibly because I was trying hard to let go and not be such an interfering parent, I mean it's not natural is it? To expect all or nothing, is such an unattractive trait, but I guess recognising it as part of my personality was a start.

Then of course, I went through the whole, 'Just be patient, he'll call when he's ready…but what if I've offended him and he's waiting for me to make contact.'

I realised that this scenario could relate itself to just about any relationship in my life, including sodding Picasso the cat, who had been visibly ignoring me in Tom's absence.

Eventually, based on the premise that I am after all still the momma, I sent Ben a text.

HI LOVE, REALLY SORRY FOR THE RANDOM TEXTS LAST NIGHT. IT HAD BEEN A LONG DAY AND I DIDN'T REALISE THE TIME! HOPE TO CATCH UP SOON.

While I was on a roll I messaged Lucy too. I resisted contacting Picasso OR Tom which I thought showed great restraint. I could do no more so I took myself off to do some grocery shopping. I called Mel to ask if they needed anything and although he only asked for milk, I made a note to replace some of the items from their supplies that had made there way into my belly over the past weeks.

As I was ploughing up the hill from town, bags laden with not so essential items, my phoned pinged a few times in succession so I plonked myself on the first available bench to check my messages.

HI MA, IF YOURE ABOUT BETWEEN 4&5 THAT WORKS FOR ME.

GREAT, THAT WORKS FOR ME TOO X

He didn't sound pissed off so that was promising.

There was also a message from Lucy.

HI THERE CASSIE, I COULD DO WITH A MEET UP SOON.
LET ME KNOW WHAT YOUR PLANS ARE OVER THE NEXT COUPLE OF WEEKS. LUCYX

ME TOO! OUT AND ABOUT RIGHT NOW, WILL CHECK CALANDER AND MESSAGE SOON. CASSxx

Then lastly from Tom;

HI CASS, I HOPE ALL IS GOOD THERE. IM HEADING BACK TO BRIGHTON TOMORROW MORNING; BE GRAND TO SEE YOU. TOM XX

HEY YOU, YES ALL FINE HERE. I SHOULD BE ABOUT LATER ON TOMORROW BUT WILL CONFIRM. I LOOK FORWARD TO HEARING ABOUT YOUR TRIP. C XX

It was good to feel connected again, albeit remotely. As I made my way slowly home, I realised just how much I missed Toms' company when he wasn't around and that was a worry, because I had no idea if I was reading the situation correctly.

By the time I had dropped the shopping round to M&M and assuaged their protests over the extra bits I had bought them, it was almost time for my call to Ben. Quickly putting away the groceries, I put the kettle on for a much needed cuppa.

'Hi Ma, I didn't read your messages till this morning. I tend to leave my phone in the kitchen at night, so you're ok, no harm done!'

It seems I hadn't read the Ben situation correctly at all. In fact, he made it clear that as we were no longer glued at the hip, (his words) he felt having our own space was perfectly healthy. It turned out that as planned, Ben, Kate, Matt and Alice had indeed found themselves a house to share and were actually in the process of moving in. As well as that, Ben had taken on some bar shifts to bump up his income for his last year at Uni. Naturally this had all been pretty time consuming.

'Well, it would have been nice to know Ben; I mean that's happened pretty quickly and I could have come and given you a hand.'

'Christ Ma, I thought you had enough on, settling into your new life; and besides the four of us managed just fine!'

'Yes of course love but my new life still needs you in it.'

'Ok Ma, can we not do this now.'

This was an indication that his patience was wearing thin. I wasn't used to this side of Ben and didn't quite know what to make of it but I managed to steer the conversation onto more mundane things and established that we should sort a date out to meet up soon.

I think Ben possibly felt that not giving into my emotion was the best way to deal with the situation, tantamount to telling me to pull myself together and back off.

Talking to Lucy later I didn't feel I could even discuss things with her as she too was behaving in an evasive manner and was very insistent that I should visit her soon.

'What's wrong with Brighton all of a sudden?'

'Well nothing Cassie, except that it is not the centre of everyone's universe. Also, you may not find time to visit once you start your new job.'

I said I would get back to her soon about dates and left it that.

I made an early dinner and poured myself a very large glass of wine. I prepared myself for a long evening of trying to figure out why it was that life had become more complicated again all of a sudden.

Who was it who said, 'The answer is not at the bottom of a glass'? Well, I'll never know because I didn't even make it halfway down the glass to ask the question. Tiredness had got the better of me and I awoke three hours later. Then I had to go through the painful process of peeling myself off the sofa, feeling stiffness in places that were not accustomed to being bent out of shape on squishy cushions for any length of time. Stumbling guiltily to bed without clearing the dishes or brushing my teeth, I knew I was going to regret it in the morning, although technically it was already morning.

Due to the dozing on the sofa, I had slept twice as long as usual, 'Well you must have needed it' I hear my mother say. With nothing to rush for I set about cleaning the flat before running a deep, scented bubble bath. I'm staring at my face in the mirror and I realise my eyes are puffy and blotchy. I don't remember crying but I must have done. I grab some thin slices of cucumber for its cooling properties and a tub of yoghurt to calm the skin, so by the time I sink into the bath I have a face that looks like a bowl of Tzatziki.

Bubbles are like wet clothing, hiding the bits you'd rather not see, but once the clothing dissolves you know it's time to get out and cover up. I have memories of Colin standing over me with that obvious look of comparison and distain on his face.

After my bath, I shower and wash my hair and emerge from the bathroom feeling like a different person and although it has taken a few gallons of water to achieve this transformation I think I recognise myself in there somewhere. 'Come on Cassie, you've got this' I had discovered over the years that during lapses of self confidence, I was very good at talking myself round.

Whilst I was preparing brunch I receive more messages.

HI MA, ARE WE OK? X

My instinct is to ask how I could possibly be ok. Then I recognise that my instinct hadn't been serving me too well recently.

HI LOVE, OF COURSE WE'RE OK. HAVE A THINK ABOUT WHEN I CAN VISIT. IT WOULD BE GOOD TO SEE THE NEW PLACE AND EVEN BETTER TO SEE YOU GUYS. HUGS MA X

GREAT! WELL WE SHOULD BE PROPERLY IN AFTER THIS WEEKEND SO LET ME KNOW WHEN MIGHT BE GOOD FOR YOU AFTER THAT. B XX

Right, well I guess that crisis may have been diverted, if I can just remember to keep my paranoia in check.

Then a message from Lucy.

CASSIE, I HAVE BEEN CHECKING DATES IN THE CALANDER AND I WAS WONDERING IF YOU MIGHT BE FREE ANY TIME OVER THE NEXT FORTNIGHT? IT WOULD BE NICE IF YOU COULD VISIT FOR A COUPLE OF DAYS, IT DOESN'T HAVE TO BE A WEEKEND. LET ME KNOW WHAT YOU THINK! LUCY X

I'm still not convinced about the change in Lucy. I feel she may be keeping something from me but I can't think what and until I know what's going on, I can't even be pissed off at her.

HEY LU, YES IM UP FOR A VISIT. I JUST NEED TO CHECK A FEW THINGS OUT BUT I WILL CALL YOU OVER THE NEXT COUPLE OF DAYS C x

I still feel a little sad but kind of back on track and I sense the coming weeks will be a busy time.

Then finally a message from Tom;

HEY YOU, JUST ARRIVED BACK IN BRIGHTON BUT WILL GO STRAIGHT TO THE GALLERY. WOULD YOU FANCY COMING BY THIS AVO? TOM xx

LOVE TO! IS THREEISH TOO EARLY? Cx

PERFECT X

I don't even care if I sound too keen, because the thought of seeing Tom seems to give me a sense of calm, as though at that moment he is the one thing that can help me straighten my head out. As I approach the gallery I have to slow my pace down when I see him, head bent over the counter, un-wrapping a piece of artwork with all the care you would give a baby. I am overcome by a huge rush of tenderness and I find myself having to restrain the impulse to rush straight to him, instead I stand quietly in the doorway, 'Hey you.'

'Hey yerself, come on in and let me look at you.' In that moment, what I saw in his face was that he had missed me too.

Within moments we were stood together in the middle of the gallery, gently kissing and holding each other as if it were the most natural thing in the world.

***

Later as we lay in Tom's bed I was at a complete loss.

'How did we get here?'

'How far back do you need me to go like? I mean I'm not that hot on the history of the cosmos '

'Ha-ha, don't start! I mean did you remember locking the gallery up when we left?'

'I should feckin' hope so! I mean as wonderfully distracted as I was, I'm able to remember the security of my properties with my eyes closed!'

'Ah so your eyes were closed, that explains how I ended up here!'

'Well I think I might just be needing a second look then!'

Later still and I wake to find I'm alone but I can just make out the sound of the shower. I quickly dress and get my stuff together and with no idea of the time I head into the kitchen for a glass of water. I am greeted by Picasso purring loudly, 'Hello lovely, I'm guessing you've been fed but I bet if I search hard enough I can find some treats. Aha, here we go.' Taking a couple of cat treat biscuits, I kneel down to stroke him. 'There we are now sweetie, it can be our little secret ok?... Except he's stood right behind me isn't he?'

Tom is smiling down at me and holding out his hand to help me up.

'This is not the first time I've found you in conversation with my cat; but I need to tell you we don't keep secrets from each other.'

'Ah, well we need to talk about that. Listen, the weather isn't looking that great so why don't I go down to mine for a shower and then make us some dinner, it is my turn after all.'

'Only if you promise, it's not going to be an evening of interrogation!'

'I promise' I kiss him and move quickly for the door 'Give me half an hour.'

Over dinner we talk about Tom's trip home, his brother Liam, Ailish's dad, had asked him over. Liam was worried about their parents and how they were coping with the running of the farm. Tom explained that there may have to be decisions made as to whether they take on more labour or sell off some of the land and live stock. Even though theirs was a large family, not all of them wanted to continue on the farm full time. 'I personally think it'll be a long while yet before those decisions need to be made but we still need to all get together with me folks and have a couple of plans in place like.'

I loved to hear him talk about his family, they were clearly very close and I said as much.

'Well, I wouldn't swap them but I'm not sure I could be living with them for too long! Anyways, what have you been up to while I was away?'

We have moved over to the sofa and leaning into him I feel very safe and comfortable, so I relay all the details of the last few days. He doesn't interrupt or make any comment until I look up at him, 'When were you going to tell me Tom?'

'Tell you?'

'Yeah, you know, about these properties you know so well with your eyes shut; about being my landlord?'

'Ah well now, as Melvin and Martha said you have to know the history to understand the present.'

It was my turn to listen. Tom told me that in the sixties when M&M were just about to take on Sanctuary House, his mammy was back in Clonakilty expecting his arrival. On January 17th 1966 he was born into the Moynihan brood. His childhood was happy and active; being the middle child he was never short of company or jobs to do on the farm. His school reports had described him as quiet and introverted. I gave him a wry smile.

'I know right? Hard to believe! I think they mistook my interest in art and Literature as some sort of issue with my development. Jaisus, I was just needing some peace in my head after being at home!'

It soon became obvious that he had a talent and reluctantly his parents agreed he could apply for Art College, providing he continued to pitch in on the farm.

'I think they thought it was more of a hobby and I'd soon grow out of it.'

Tom went on to gain a degree in fine arts at the National College of Art and Design in Dublin. ' Growing up in Clon, I was always going to be drawn to seascapes and countryside but I'd had a taste of city life at College and I was keen to find out what else was on offer.'

I think I saw him blush a little when he mentioned that he had followed a girlfriend to London where they lived together for five years.

'What happened?'

'Usual I guess. We wanted different things and to be honest I was tiring of London. I very nearly went home that year but I wanted to check out the English coastline first. So I took myself off for a year, teaching kids at Art projects and the like.'

That's how he had met M&M. They were struggling to keep the Drama Academy going and they were letting out rooms and teaching space in a building that Tom had felt an immediate connection to.

'So wait, that was around 1997?'

'That'd be about right'

'Tom, you've lived here for 16 years?'

'Give or take, I guess so, with a lot of coming and going in between.'

So much had happened during those 16 years. Once Tom had decided to stay in Brighton he had already learnt of Martha's illness which had been diagnosed 10 years previously. It was clear that they would continue to struggle as time went on.

'More than anything, I didn't want them to lose their home, especially when they had given so much to so many. They had been really supportive of me, a bit like another Ma and Da you know, except that we were connected by our interest in the Arts.'

Over the following five years on his trips back to Ireland he would tell his family all about M&M and Sanctuary House. His parents even made the trip over to 'see what all the fuss was about' and found they formed a bond straight away. Meanwhile, Tom carried on taking on students but also began showing and selling some of his work which was why he rented the Boardwalk Gallery.

'Then in 2002 my Granda passed and life changed completely. Aw Cassie, what a fella, big in stature and big in heart, everyone just thought he would go on forever. Sure he was just after celebrating his 100th birthday! Anyways, god rest him, he made sure that each and everyone of us kids inherited a sum of money with the strict instructions that we did whatever we saw fit with our share. I'm pretty sure he knew what I'd be doing with mine.'

'You bought Sanctuary House?' I asked in disbelief.

It hadn't been quite as simple as that and a lot of planning and negotiations were involved. Basically, Tom had bought the whole building from Melvyn and Martha on the understanding that he would renovate it to its former glory but at the same time converting the space to provide 4 flats. M&M would remain in their ground floor flat and it would be altered to their specifications, Tom would have his glorious loft space and the remaining two flats would provide a steady income. As it happened, when Ray came along he wasn't interested in renting but was keen to buy and also be involved in the renovation. This added more money to the pot for the work. That left just one flat as a rental property which is where I fitted in.

Tom broke the silence. 'A lot to take in isn't it darlin'?'

'Just a bit! I'm also curious though; I mean this beautiful building has obviously been a labour of love over the past 10 years but how did that affect the rest of your life?'

'You know something, that time has just flown by; it's been full on and in the main, exciting. Mel, Martha and me, you know it gave us a sense of purpose. The building had provided everything it could over the years and it was a bit like saying thank you....coaxing her back to life. It couldn't be rushed; we wanted to do her justice you know?'

'Her?'

'Yeah the building, she's special and needed to be treated with respect! Mind it wouldn't have taken quite so long if ordinary life hadn't got in the way. I know what you are wanting to know Cass and you nailed it on the head when you said the house was a labour of love. Don't misunderstand me, I have had a few relationships over the years and I really tried to make it work, but none of them got me. None of them were special enough or crazy enough to understand me or any of all this.'

'Oh, so am I crazy enough for you then?'

'So far, you've got craziness in spades and quite cute with it too, now I can't be asking for more than that now can I?'

[24]

I'd slept like a baby; literally, I woke with my head on Tom's chest with his arms cradled around me.

'Tom?' I croaked

'You're not going to ask how we got here again are you' He sounded wide awake.

'No... but I was thinking you must be really uncomfortable!'

'I'll let you know once I get the feeling back in my arms like'

'Oh god, did I snore?'

'I'd call it more a gentle purring.'

'Are you sure Picasso isn't in here with us?'

'Lucky cat'

'Seriously Tom, I was thinking,'

'When?'

'When what?'

'When was you thinking; I mean you've been looking real peaceful for the last hour or so.' He exaggerated the discomfort of his arms. I laughed and gently unwrapped myself.

'Better?'

'Much. So why so serious girl?'

'I was just wondering if we ought to pop down to see Mel and Martha today'

'That sounds a grand idea; and what else?'

'Sorry?'

'What else is on your mind?'

'Just stuff'

'You might have to be more specific Cass'

'I'm scared'

He plumped up the pillows as if he needed more blood to the brain for this conversation.

'Of what exactly?'

'This—us, my changing relationships with other people, the new job....doesn't it scare you?'

'Nope, they're your fears Cass. I never get scared of anything that hasn't proved itself to me. Jaisus girl, nothing in this life stands still and you can't spoil the good times waiting for the worst that might never happen! I'm not Colin darlin' and I see something in you that I would like in my life – if I can take a leap of faith you can too. I'm no angel and you might turn out to be a right pain in the backside but what do we lose by finding out? And all that other stuff? Well that's where it helps being the two of us.'

Dear god please don't let me say anything too ridiculous, I lean over to kiss him,

'I think I just got a glimpse of your angelic side.'

'Well you'll not be seeing it for long if you don't let me up the stairs for a shower and a change of clothes!'

He turned at the door and winked at me, 'See you in a bit love'

One hour later and we were stood outside Em and Em's door, Tom puts his key in the lock, opens the door slightly and shouted out, 'Are youse decent? It's only us!'

It doesn't register until he grabs my hand that he is announcing us both.

'Come in, come in darlings!'

With a smile and a wink he gently propels me into the sitting room where Mel and Martha are waiting. I can actually feel the excitement in the room as they hug and greet us like long lost family. Amidst all the chatter, Mel is directing us to sit on the sofa, all the while informing us that the coffee is on! I feel a little overwhelmed but in a good way. Tom hands a bag over to Martha, 'From me Ma with love. A drop of the good stuff and one of her Barmbracks.'

'Oh, how lovely, please tell her thank you kindly! Mel perhaps we could take a slice of the cake with coffee?'

Tom gets up to give Mel a hand.

'If you need any more shopping I can nip into town today.'

'Oh, no thank you Tom, Cassie brought us such a lovely selection of groceries yesterday.'

'Did she now?' he smiled and sat back next to me.

We spent a lovely hour or so, shooting the breeze, as Mel called it; we discussed the idea of having a house BBQ now that Spring was easing into Summer. M&M seemed happy to take on the task of pinning Ray and Andy down to a date. I cleared the coffee dishes and took them through to the kitchen; Mel followed me through singing softly to himself. Then Tom and I took our leave and as we closed the door behind us, I sighed in relief, Tom pulled me to him 'See that wasn't so bad now was it?'

'No, it was rather lovely actually.'

Tom went down to the gallery to start planning his exhibition for September and I went up to organise dates for my visits to Cardiff and Surrey but we decided to meet later for a drink.

Back in my flat, things felt different, there was an extra layer of warmth, a feeling of two and yes it was scary, but I liked it.

I looked at suitable dates but I hesitated to confirm anything. I took myself out for some head space with a walk towards the Marina; on my way back Tom messaged to say he was in town and would I fancy meeting in the pub. The very same pub we'd had our first 'date' in.

As he brought the drinks over, I commented, 'This is a bit surreal; I mean the last time we were here was barely two weeks ago, yet so much has happened since then!'

'Indeed it has' he bent to kiss my forehead before sitting opposite me 'so I thought we should eat out tonight by way of celebration'

'Sounds great! As long as we don't go anywhere too swanky, since I've just come from a long walk! I probably should check how my finances are holding up too.'

'Jais, but other than that it sounds great right? Firstly, you look gorgeous, secondly its my treat and thirdly…swanky…is that even a proper word?'

'Firstly thank you for the compliment, secondly that's very kind of you to treat me, I'll buy the next round and thirdly, yes it is indeed a word; swanky—an informal adjective meaning, luxurious and expensive.'

'Ah, you mean fancy! Did you just Google that? Anyways I'm too Bohemian to go 'swanky' remember?'

Banter finally done, I explained to Tom that my walk had been a delay tactic on coming to decisions about my visits.

'I wasn't sure if you might like to come with me?'

116

There was no response to this question.

'Did I say the wrong thing?'

'Hush girl, I'm thinking.'

'Dangerous'

'Now here's the thing. That's quite a decision. Not for me, I'll go anywhere with you, but for you Cass, I mean it must have taken some time to think on that.'

'Not really. It just felt right.'

'Ok. Well if you don't mind me suggesting, maybe you should ask how it sits with everyone else before you make your decision. Especially Ben. Then if you still want me to come with you that's grand, but don't buy train tickets, I'll drive us.' He calmly sips his Guinness while watching for my reaction.

'You have a car?'

That wicked smile is going to finish me.

We end up going to a Bistro in the Lanes. Tom tells me all about his plans for his Dublin exhibition and that his old college have invited him to give some lectures to run at the same time. As well as that there was talk of a couple of commissions that were under discussion.

'Wow Tom that's amazing! No wonder you wanted to celebrate.'

'These past few weeks have been pretty special that's for sure'

'Listen, you've got such a lot going on, please don't let me be a distraction, you know I'll understand if you need to step back a bit.'

'Feckin' crazy woman! Listen, things are going to get busy for both of us in the Autumn, I've already got Ailish lined up to give a hand in the gallery over the Summer. So—unless you're quitting on me already, stepping back's not an option darlin'.'

On the slow walk home after dinner, I suggest that in all seriousness we should not stay together every night in case it compromised other areas of our relationship. Stopping in his tracks he turned me to face him, 'On the other hand, we could just behave like grown ups and go with the flow like? I mean I'm pretty sure that's how adult relationships develop—or not. Look, I'm happy to try it your way love if that's what you really want, but maybe just not tonight OK?'

117

There was really no arguing with him on that point.

[25]

The next morning I called Lucy on the off chance I would catch her at home.

'Hi Lucy, is this a bad time?'

There was a slight delay and an intake of breath.

'No, no it's fine, I'm not going anywhere till later'

'Oh good, I won't keep you but I just wanted to ask you if you were free for me to come visit next Wednesday? Just for a couple of nights, till Friday maybe?'

'Ah, let me just grab my diary.'

The conversation felt very stilted as though Lucy was playing for time.

'So next Wednesday, let me see now. Yes that looks doable, perhaps you could give me an idea of times once you've booked your ticket?'

'Yeah, of course, but I also wanted to ask how you would feel about Tom coming along?'

The silence was so palpable I could barely breathe. In the absence of an instant response I felt I already had my answer so to save any further embarrassment I said,

'Although, you and I haven't had much time to ourselves lately so perhaps Tom could come another time.'

'Goodness Cassie, you two seem to have got serious very quickly! Yeah, maybe another time would be better if you don't mind'

Something was very wrong here but there was no way I wanted to be having this conversation on the phone so I tried to remain upbeat.

'No problem at all, I'll get on and book my tickets and let you know the details as soon as possible! It'll be so good to catch up Luce, can I bring anything?'

'Ha, well, we're not short of shops here Cassie, so I'm sure we'll be fine but thanks for asking.'

'Lucy, that's not what I meant silly, I just...

'Sorry Cass, there's someone at the door with a delivery, so I must go, but look forward to seeing you soon!'

She had hung up before I had time to answer. Well that was not at all pleasant. Instead of dwelling on the whys and what ifs, I got on and booked my tickets for the following Wednesday to return early on the Friday. I sent the times to Lucy, she replied, IN THE DIARY X

I then messaged Ben and to my surprise he called straight back.

'Hi Ma, how you doing?'

'Hya love, I wasn't sure you would be about.'

'Yeah, we're just moving the last few things in today so as from now we are the official new tenants!'

'Yey, that's great! I know what a good feeling that is! Listen, I wondered if you'd be up for a visit next weekend?'

'Don't see why not Ma, let me just check with the guys…'

'Erm before you do that; would you be up for Tom coming as well?'

'Yeah, that'd be amazing, the more the merrier! I'm assuming you guys will be ok in the spare room?'

The role reversal wasn't lost on me.

'Well if you're cool with that son, thanks.'

The chuckling in the background indicated we were on speaker phone. It was so good to hear that at least Ben was back to his old self and it lifted my mood. I would feel so much better once I knew what was going on with Lucy but I would have to be patient.

Tom was working upstairs in his studio for the day. I messaged him to tell him I would be making dinner that evening and he was welcome to join me later if he was free. When I opened the door to him I smiled at the evidence of his days labours,

'You're a match for Picasso cat' I laughed ruffling his paint splattered hair.

'Yeah sorry about that, will I go shower first?'

'No, I quite like it—it maintains the boho look!'

'Well, this bohemian is starving and something smells great!'

Over dinner I told Tom about all the arrangements I'd made and how concerned I was about Lucy's behaviour.

'Ah darlin' I'm thinking she needs proper time with you on your own and sure you'll find out soon enough what the bother is. I'm real chuffed about Ben like; it'll be good to see him and his mates again.'

'Yeah, it sounded like they were all looking forward to seeing us too.'

After dinner we went for an evening walk. The sky was beautifully clear and the stars so bright that they spread a celestial canopy over the calm ocean. We sat on the sea wall looking out at the vastness of it all and Tom hugged me to him.

'I forgot to say, we've been officially invited to the house BBQ this Sunday.'

'Wow, two weekend invites in a row, I guess that makes us a couple. Serious huh?'

'I would say so.'

'Do you mind?'

'I'm thinking it's a bit late for minding. How about you?'

'I mind enough to be thinking I should be getting you a spare key cut.'

'Don't be wasting your cash love; I already have one.'

'Ah, of course you do. I'm surprised you haven't used it yet!'

'Shame on you girl, what do you take me for.'

There had been a little rain during the night on the Saturday but it looked like Sunday would be perfect BBQ weather. Everyone was due to gather in the garden around lunchtime so I had left Tom working that morning to go shopping. I wanted to make some salads and a pudding to contribute to the meal.

It felt like a long time since I had seen Ray and Andy, apart from a fleeting hello in passing, so I was really looking forward to catching up with them.

Carrying a tray of salads and a bottle of wine in a bag over my shoulder, I made my way carefully down the stairs. The door to the garden was propped open so I could already hear the mixed chatter of the now familiar voices; the smell of slow burning charcoal cut through the wonderful scent of earthy petrichor created by the previous night's rain. The lazy laughter

121

made me smile and as I stepped into the garden I wished I had my camera to capture the scene.

Andy and Ray were each tending a BBQ and looking resplendent in matching floral aprons; the long wooden table at the centre of the garden was decorated with wild flowers and candles. There was an eclectic mix of seating adorned with plump cushions and throws. The magical sound of Miles Davies was drifting through the air, creating a soulful ambience.

Mel and Martha were sat holding hands and smiling broadly at something Tom was relaying to them. I felt frozen on the threshold for a short time, then suddenly they all looked up at once and the moment moved on.

Tom rushed over, 'You should have called me to come and help love, what were you thinking carrying this lot down the feckin' stairs?'

'I was thinking I would prove that I'm not in the habit of tripping over every obstacle in my way!'

'That's my girl, you look gorgeous by the way' and in one fell swoop he had kissed me and relieved me of the tray I was carrying, much to the delight of the onlookers who let out a cheer.

'Now come on you lot, I feel like a celebrity!'

Ray hugged me, 'Well you look like one darling, my goodness Cass you're glowing lady!'

'See, didn't I tell you this would happen if you stayed here' Andy planted a kiss on my cheek.

'Cut it out Mystic Meg, I can't take you seriously in that apron! Let me help take the food to the table.'

The last time we had all gathered together, was at my flat warming and I remember wondering then, how it was possible to feel such a strong connection with this rich mix of people who I barely knew. Yet here we were again, just the six of us, having the best afternoon ever. There was an honesty and warmth in our conversation, good food, fine wine and so much laughter.

When I slipped away to bring dessert from the fridge, Tom was close behind me.

'Wait, I'll give you a hand.'

'Great, thanks; it's only Eton Mess and it literally is one big mess, so I'm hoping no one will notice!'

'I think you could give them Clonakilty Custard and they'd be just as happy!'

'It's lovely isn't it? This is how I imagine being part of a proper family feels like.'

'Careful what you wish for love'

'Clonakilty custard, you just made that up didn't you? Here you take spoons and dishes and I'll bring the mess.'

The afternoon blended into early evening and although there was still some daylight left we lit the candles and opened another bottle of wine. Tom and I walked Em and Em indoors when they felt ready to call it a day and making sure they were comfortable, we then returned to the garden for one last drink with the boys.

Climbing the stairs together Tom turned to me, 'Your place or mine?'

'Mines closer'

'Sure, yours it is then.'

[26]

Wednesday morning brought mixed feelings; I hadn't been back to Surrey since I left in March, which seemed a lifetime ago. Tom offered to walk with me to the station but I hate good byes so I told him to go create.

'Fair enough but be in touch yeah?'

It wasn't a long journey but I had two changes, so I settled in to try and relax on the first part which took me to London. I loved travelling by train, especially when I was alone as I could watch the world go by and lose myself in a good book or my own thoughts. Lucy was probably right; in that I had been totally self absorbed the last couple of months; but surely I couldn't help the speed of events. I also remembered how excited she had seemed for me, encouraging me to enjoy all that Brighton had to offer, including my relationship with Tom.

There had been no offer of a lift from the station so when we eventually pulled in to Guildford, I had the sudden urge to get the next available train back home; 'home' because that's where your heart is right?

Lucy lived on the outskirts of town so I got a taxi to her house and now standing outside the door I started to worry that I wouldn't be welcome.

The door opened and my heart leapt to my throat, a shadow of my dearest friend stood before me, the remnants of a yellowing bruise around her eye.

'No! Fuck no!' I cried out and pulled her to me to stop her racking sobs and to control my own body from shaking. I was holding her so tightly I was scared of hurting her further but she was pleading with me to come inside, her eyes casting up and down the street for fear of being seen or of what she may see. Inside we went directly to the kitchen where I made her sit while I put the kettle on. Tea- the go to for any crisis and the amount of tea Lucy and I had got through over the years meant that we could make each other the perfect cup without asking. Out of my rucksack I produced a little box of lemon and poppy seed muffins, 'When in doubt eat cake!' I was rewarded with the faintest of smiles but it took a while to coax her to quit the small talk and tell me what had happened.

For as long as I had known Lucy, she had enjoyed photography, so it came as no surprise when she joined a local class to improve her hobby. I think she had already been attending the weekly class for a few months before I left for Brighton. It was a fairly small group of between six and eight like minded people getting together once a week to learn new skills and discuss their work. I knew she was enjoying it because she always became very animated when we met in the days following her class. I thought the reason she never mentioned her fellow students was because she was too engrossed in all that she was learning from the course. However, there was one guy called Simon who Lucy felt she got on really well with; pretty soon they were meeting outside the group for walks in the surrounding countryside.

'How long Luce?'

'I guess from the start of the course, but it didn't get serious till the beginning of March.'

I was staring at her incredulously.

'So, what happened to our golden rule, you know... the one that I made sure I kept to when I went anywhere on my own?'

I really didn't want to upset her, but I was so angry.

'I know, and I am truly sorry Cassie; I don't know what I was thinking, but you had a lot going on and...'

'Hush, lets not talk about that now, just tell me what happened.'

Apparently, Simon had been really 'attentive and kind' and they began to meet several times a week but always at Lucy's place, never at his and if they met at the pub with the group he asked her not to reveal their relationship 'just yet'.

'Once, I asked why he didn't talk about his background' he seemed genuinely upset and revealed that following a messy divorce from 'the wicked wife from the west' he was living in a grotty bed sit and was too embarrassed to tell anyone. Then a couple of weeks back I asked him to come with me to Brighton to visit my dearest friend and her new partner.' The tears came again and I sat next to her with my arm around her shoulders. 'I thought he would enjoy going somewhere different and even offered to pay for a hotel if he was too shy to stay at yours. He was so angry.'

'So... no grotty bed sit and no wicked wife?'

Lucy put her head in her hands but when I uncovered her face I was trembling,

'Did he do this?'

She was obviously reluctant to respond.

'Luce, did that bastard do this?'

She nodded, 'He told me that I'd be sorry if I ever told anyone about our fling and did I seriously think he would leave his wife and home for me. He was gripping my arm so tightly, I got scared and I asked him to leave before I called the police, that was when he struck me, but of course he blamed me for making him angry.'

'Of course he did the spineless bastard! Where does this shit live Luce?'

Another hint of a smile.

'Don't you worry Cass...the boys were on it straight away, he is now in the process of being charged for assault. There is a restraining order in place and while I don't imagine he would have the guts to come near me, I don't trust him to adhere to it.'

It transpires that 'simple Simon' had failed to recognise that Lucy was a force to be reckoned with, especially with the love and support of two strapping sons.

'I was so angry and humiliated Cass, there was no way he was going to get away with it, also as sad as I felt for his wife, she needed to know too.'

'Well I am so glad you told the boys straight away, I bet they were well and truly pissed!'

We ordered a take out for dinner, opened a bottle of wine and talked at length well into night. It was so obvious now why Lucy had distanced herself from me and although I was still a little hurt, I understood all the reasoning behind her behaviour.

'So what will you do now?'

'Ah, I've got some more news for you..sorry.'

'What?'

'The house is on the market. No matter what happens to Simon, I can't stay here Cass. William is buying a house in

France and has asked me to move with him while I decide what to do next. The further away the better for the moment.'

I was more relieved than shocked. I knew she would be safe with William and there would be plenty of time for her to think about her future plans.

'I think I can manage a trip to France now and then!'

It was late when we turned in but I was heartened that we had finished the evening excitedly chatting about France.

Lying in bed, I checked a message from Tom.

HEY LOVE, GLAD YOURE THERE SAFE. NOT EXPECTING A REPLY BUT HOPE ALL IS OK. MISSING YOU A LITTLE TOO MUCH.XX

HEY YOU, VERY INTENSE HERE, WORDS ARE FAILING ME (SHOCKER HUH?) BUT WORKING OUR WAY THROUGH IT. I'M HOPING I'LL GET A DECENT SLEEP BUT I MISS YOU TOO.XX

I woke early and had to really focus my mind. I felt somewhat disorientated being in a different bed without Tom beside me. How quickly we become accustomed to that which gives us comfort. Then a huge sense of sadness for Lucy brought a lump to my throat. I looked in on her and she was sleeping soundly so I showered and dressed. I pottered in the kitchen for a while and then made a cup of tea to take upstairs.

'Hey Luce, I brought you a cuppa. When you're ready, I'll get some breakfast on the go.'

'Great, down in a bit.' She mumbled.

Lucy shuffled into the kitchen half an hour later wearing a dressing gown that swamped her decreasing frame.

'How long have you been up?'

'Ages and I'm starving! What can I tempt you with?'

'Just coffee for now'

'Ok, I'll put a bit of toast on in case you change your mind. Sorry but I need some fuel,' I was chucking in the fruit and yoghurt as if I hadn't eaten for weeks.

'You do look really good Cass and I'm so pleased things are going well for you.'

I was struggling and she knew it.

'You are allowed to tell me you're happy you know.'
'I am happy Luce...but not when I see you like this. How about we hit the shops today?'
'Not today Cass, honestly, I'll be fine once I'm away from here and that wont be long. Will is coming tomorrow to help me pack up and then I'm out of here.'
'In that case, today we will have a home spa day; you need to look your best for when William comes tomorrow. You have a bit of toast or what ever; I'm just nipping to the chemist for some face packs!'
After a morning of pure pampering I sent Lucy to soak in the bath while I made lunch which I set up in the garden, she emerged looking much more rested and we spent a lovely afternoon discussing her future plans.
'Promise me two things. Firstly, you will never again feel that you can't reach out to me; secondly, no matter where we are, we will always get to each other and also, as soon as you are physically able, you go to the hairdressers!'
'Well typically, that's three things but it's a deal'
When the time came to leave on Friday morning I felt drained but more settled. William had arrived early and also Steven was following on later; there was safety in numbers. William was giving me a lift to the station but Lucy had declined to come along for the ride, we had a long hug before I left.
'Thanks Cass, I'm feeling so much stronger and much more positive now.'
'Make sure you stay that way my friend.'

Outside the station Will turned to me,
'Mum wouldn't let us tell you Cassie. She said it was because you had a lot going on but I think she felt really embarrassed.'
'Oh, I know that Will; but I also knew that whatever was going on she needed time. Your mum and I go back a long way, but our kids have always been our first port of call, sorry and all that! Take good care of her for me wont you and please stay in touch.'

On the journey into London a sudden wave of emotion came over me, so I put on my shades and huddled next to the cooling window to allow for a few tears. I watched the Surrey countryside disappear along with a part of my life that I had no problems letting go of once and for all, and I was pretty sure that Lucy would feel the same once she left it all behind.

Taking my seat on the Brighton train, I allowed the comforting rhythm of the tracks to calm me, I was so grateful to be heading home. When I got off at the station, I was thinking to stop for a coffee to reboot my failing energy. I cast my eyes around the forecourt looking for a coffee shop but I immediately saw Tom, standing with his hands in his pockets, just waiting for me to find the comfort in his hug, ' Welcome back Cass.'

We walked back along the front and I felt the healing properties of the sea air. Tom let me talk until I thought I could talk no more and when we reached my flat he opened the door.

'Do you want some time alone love?'

'No- please stay, being alone is the last thing I want right now.'

So we shared the brunch that Tom had bought, and then he gently helped me into our bed and held me till I fell asleep.

I awoke in the middle of the afternoon to find a beautiful bouquet of flowers on the kitchen counter with a note.

Cass, I'm down at the gallery handing over to Ailish for the weekend. Rest up darlin', I'll be back later xx

I felt a little selfish to be thinking how lucky I was that I had a Tom and not a Simon.

[27]

As I am not a driver, I am very aware of what an awful passenger I must be. If anyone is kind enough to offer me transport, I will do my utmost to direct them along 'B' roads and country lanes to avoid a motorway; even if taking the scenic route adds an extra 45 minutes to the journey. Failing that I can spend the whole trip gripping the edge of my seat till my knuckles turn white and by the end of the journey, my teeth have been so tightly clenched, I can taste the amalgam from my fillings. When Tom had blithely informed me that Brighton to Cardiff would involve three and a half hours of motorway travel, I must have visibly paled.

'If we get an early start we can stop for breakfast—to break the journey like.'

He then went on to reassure me that he had taken the car to the garage while I was at Lucy's' and had done all the usual checks;

'Tyre pressure, fuel, electrics, ejector seats… so we're good to go!'

So it was reassuring that I felt so relaxed when we accessed the M4 from London to Cardiff. There may have been several reasons for my soporific attitude; firstly, having left home at 7.00 a.m. I had yet to fully emerge from my slumberous state and had not yet had my caffeine hit. Secondly, I had already observed that Tom was a very competent and considerate driver, not once had I felt the need to slam my feet on the imaginary brakes and I couldn't believe we were already halfway through our journey. Lastly, Tom owned a tank; well not literally but knowing nothing about cars, I was taken aback when we arrived at the lock-up garage that morning to be greeted by a Land Rover which was rather aptly named DEFENDER.

'Wow Tom, we could have a party in here!'

'Yeah, it probably seems a bit excessive but I mainly use it for going home to help out on the farm and that.'

It was evident what its main purpose was, as the outside was artistically splattered with good Irish muck.

'All your own work?' I smiled

'Aye sorry about that, but I did clean up the inside.'

'No, I like it.'

So, wrapped in this huge cocoon of a car, we wend our way to Cardiff and when we stopped for coffee and a comfort break, I messaged Ben. Thankfully, he told me that there was a hotel at the end of their road where we could pay for 24 hour parking.

The journey had been smooth and relaxed; we had chatted and sang badly most of the way so that by the time we arrived 4 hours later I felt fully awake.

'Thank you driver'

'Thank you passenger'

While we were taking our overnight bags from the car, we were laughing at the fact that our house warming gifts seemed to consist mainly of booze with the obligatory house plant; 'I blame the parent' laughed Tom.

I looked past him and saw Ben walking towards us, I knew it was highly unlikely but I thought he had grown.

'Blimey Ma, you weren't joking about the tank!' he was shaking Tom's hand comfortably whilst admiring DEFENDER at the same time.

'Nice to see you too love'

'Sorry Ma, you look well!' then straight in with the Ben hug.

As we clinked our way merrily up the hill, I commented on what a lovely road it was, tree lined with a view of the Cardiff hills in the distance.

'Yep, and we're right at the top so it saves on gym membership'

I'm not quite sure what I was expecting but I guess from my past experiences, I still had the ramshackle student rooms at the forefront of my mind. This house was far from that. It was a lovely Victorian terrace with two bedrooms and the luxury of an upstairs bathroom; then downstairs were two reception rooms, one of which doubled as a study and third bedroom. There was a reasonable size kitchen that had been extended out to accommodate a dining table and chairs; this led onto a small patio space at the back of the building.

'Ben this is so lovely and they obviously decorated just before you moved in'

'Ah, well we decided to go private rent rather than the student accommodation route. We were really lucky; the landlord liked the look of us and our finances!'

Tom was nodding his approval,

'Definitely worth going for, especially when you can share the expense.'

'Yeah, well Mattie's the accountant so he'll be keeping us on our toes. Now how about a cuppa?'

When Ben went to put the kettle on I whispered to Tom,

'It's a proper grown up house.'

'Ah, don't be sad love; the boyo is on his way, you should be really proud.'

Matt, Alice and Kate arrived back from shopping carrying a multitude of groceries. They seemed genuinely excited to be entertaining their first house guests.

'We couldn't decide what to get for dinner so we've gone for a kind of mezze platter with salads' Kate enthused.

'Ooh great choice'

That afternoon we all went for a walk to Sophia Park and Gardens where we sat by the river. I mentioned how strange it was that although I had visited Cardiff many times, I had never really explored the area and that I could sense the city had many hidden gems.

'Well to be fair ma, it has usually been pretty rubbish weather. Next time, you guys should come for a bit longer and we can give you a proper city tour, there's a lot more to see.'

Tom had slipped his hand in mine,

'That'd be grand Ben, thanks, its great when some one can show you the best an area has on offer.'

I just caught Ben's eye as he sent a hint of a nod my way.

Over dinner we discussed all the merits of there just being the four of them sharing. I got the distinct feeling they had already moved on from their student days and that this last year would be a time for growing as well as working towards individual goals. Tom and I then shared the potted version of

132

M&M's story, which they found fascinating and heart rending in equal measure. We touched on future plans and where we might all be come Christmas.

'Hey, but let's not wish the year away!'

We all raised a glass to that.

Later, as we lay on our comfy sofa bed, I asked Tom how he felt the day had gone.

'I think it's been great—our first weekend away together to meet the parents.'

'Ha-ha, well I think you've been given the seal of approval, so we'd best not blot our copy books.'

'Which means?'

'Well let's just say it means we have to behave ourselves.'

'Well now that's a crying shame.'

Sunday morning and Tom and I were up and about before the kids. We took a cup of tea onto the patio while the sun still shone. When everyone else finally surfaced, we suggested taking a walk up to the castle to have a late breakfast out.

'Our treat, as a thank you for having us!'

As we were planning on travelling back around three it was a good opportunity to get a walk in and spend more time with them all before we left.

I managed to have a short chat with Ben alone and I told him about Lucy; he was visibly shaken, 'Well he sounds a prize twat. Poor Lucy, I'm glad Will and Steve have it in hand.'

'Oh me too; it was so sad to see her in such a state Ben' I was still getting choked talking about it.

'Well, she'll be looked after now Ma. Look... I know it's been a difficult few weeks, but I hope you know I'll always look out for you. Tom seems a really decent bloke, so I'm pretty sure you won't be needing me in that way; but just so as you know.'

'Ditto' I smiled nudging him.

Back in Brighton, Tom and I took an evening walk along the front. Breathing in the air and linking arms, I sighed happily and looked up at a well timed murmuration,

'What a lovely weekend that was, but its still great to be home, I really like it here Tom.'

'Yeah, it's a pretty good place; especially right now' he pulled me towards him, 'Do you think we could stop behaving though?'

'Oh I don't see why not.'

The evening light signalled that summer was already well on its way, and although I desperately wanted the feeling to last, I knew it was time to stop treating it like a long holiday; time to see if reality bites.

[28]

I rang Professor Bennet at the University the next morning to see if I could possibly visit campus that day, it was now late May and I was aware that June would get busy as this was the end of the Summer term for undergraduates. It was so difficult keeping up with all the different dates and though September seemed a tantalizingly long way off I really needed to fit in a few visits before then. After a short while on hold the secretary came back to me, 'Miss Peters, so sorry to have kept you, I knew Professor Bennet was unavailable today but I know Imani is eager to meet you, would you be able to come in around 10.45?'

Of course, I couldn't say no but I was immediately nervous at the prospect of meeting someone new. Imani Okeke was my immediate boss but I had yet to meet her as she had been unable to attend my interviews due to a family commitment. I decided to take the bus rather than cycle as I didn't want to risk meeting Imani in a sweaty crumpled heap.

The school of Arts and Media was based in Moulsecomb campus and the 25 minute bus ride wasn't really providing the calming affect I had hoped for, I felt like a new student myself which I suppose, technically I was. I remembered in my teens, revisiting my primary school and marvelling at how tiny everything was and wondering why it had all been so very scary; well this was the polar opposite. The campus was so much bigger than I remembered and I felt I had every right to be terrified. I had a sudden throwback to that doctors' office in Surrey which seemed an eternity ago now, but I felt the familiar prickling sensation on my skin and the bitter taste creeping its nasty way into my salivary ducts. Jeez Cassandra, get a grip! I had arrived at my destination with time to spare so I was practicing my deep breathing mantra when I was suddenly aware I had no idea where I was going. The mantra was soon forgotten and quickly replaced by a less salubrious chant as I navigated my way to Student Support Services (the irony wasn't lost on me) but I did eventually find myself outside Imani's office.

I was immediately put at ease when she greeted me.

'Ah Cassie; welcome to Moulsecoomb! Do you mind if we grab a coffee before we start? I'm gasping!'

The first thing that struck me about Imani was her lovely genuine smile; followed closely by the array of amazing colours she was wearing from her head wrap down to her Harem style trousers; a stunning collection of Batik fabrics which would have put Joseph's coat to shame. I followed her down a corridor where we got coffee at a vending machine and found a seat in a quiet study area.

'I can't begin to tell you how grateful I am that you have popped by today, it makes my job so much easier come the start of term if I've been able to give a rough idea of what makes us tick.'

I had only intended to stay for an hour or two but four hours later we were sat having lunch in the concourse. I had learnt so much from my visit but I was sure I would have missed a lot of details. I had noticed a few times that Imani had slowed her pace, giving me time to jot some notes down and now she was eyeing my notebook with curiosity.

'Oh, I'm so sorry about my copious note taking; I can't even blame my age, I've always been a scribbler, 'post-its' have made a small fortune out of me over the years!

I am perfectly happy with technology but I've always relied on the written word to make sense to me and I find a combination of the two gives me perfect clarity, I'm sure no one else would understand it though!'

'Oh on the contrary Cassie, I get it completely,' she grinned, 'I am a great fan of the written word my self, I think it shows an enthusiasm for knowledge.'

Imani walked with me to the exit.

'You know Cassie, it is perfectly normal to feel overwhelmed coming into this environment and although we have covered a lot today, don't expect to remember it all. Never feel you can't come to me or indeed any of your colleagues with questions, in fact I would be concerned if you didn't! Also, don't forget you will be shadowing the team for a couple of months at least.'

'Poor them' I laughed holding up my notebook.

'You'll be absolutely fine and I am very much looking forward to working with you in September.'

I left the campus feeling drained but remarkably upbeat; Imani had managed to give me a sense of worth which I realised had been sadly missing in some of my previous jobs. Later I excitedly relayed my visit to Tom.

'Well sure she sounds great, see now didn't I say not to worry? So how old is Imani?'

'Do you know, I have no idea; she has one of those beautiful, timeless faces, full of wisdom with not a wrinkle to show for it.'

We sat together on the balcony and googled Imani Okeke. I was really surprised to discover she was 10 years my senior but when I read her list of achievements and how highly respected she was in her field of Arts and humanities I was astounded that anyone would have the time to fit so much academia into a lifetime. Not only that but she was an established author on the history of African culture.

'Blimey no wonder she is a fan of the written word, she has more letters after her name than alphabetti spaghetti, Dr Okeke is one amazing lady!'

I had such admiration for women like Omani but having met her, I didn't feel intimidated in the least and I finally felt confident about starting work again.

[29]

I wasn't entirely sure what was bugging me. I mean other than the fact that I didn't appear to have anything to worry about at the moment. I suppose the fact that my life in the past had been so vastly different, meant that I didn't have a clue whether this was classed as normal or not. Life had slid into a perfectly comfortable routine. Aside from the every day tasks that I assumed everyone has to fit into their lifestyle, I also managed to take a daily walk or bike ride; and on several occasions I visited the University to further enhance that feeling of belonging I had received at my meeting with Imani. Some times, I would drop in on Mel and Martha, I was always rewarded with a wonderful hour or more of chat and much needed advice and of course if I timed it right, the obligatory coffee and cake.

'I am going to miss this so much when I start work.'

'Indeed, as will we Cassie, but you can always drop in after work if you're not too tired and there are always the weekends.'

Martha sounded quite sad so I added, 'Ooh and of course I will have some time off during the holidays.' However, there was no denying that it wouldn't be the same.

Andy and Ray were their usual elusive selves so not much change there but we still managed to meet in the garden some weekends or we might bump into them in the pub. They were full of local information and gossip and they would try unsuccessfully to get me to divulge secrets.

'We give up Cassie, you are way too discreet! No fun at all!'

Lucy and I maintained regular contact and we were hoping to fit in a weekend visit before she moved to France with Will and his partner by the end of the year.

'Wow, Christmas in a whole other country Luce, and I thought I was brave!'

'I know, but I also remember how excited you were Cassie, and I think I get it now.'

It was a comfort to me that she was sounding so much better and relishing the idea of change, I remembered that feeling well; after all it was only a little while ago that I was plotting my own escape.

Ben and I would often text during the week but we always made time for a video call on a Friday evening or over the weekend, he was always very upbeat and was gearing up for his final academic year. Time that elusive thief.

Tom's niece, Ailish had been helping in the gallery part of the summer holidays so she was using his flat as a base, which meant Tom had moved in with me. I adored waking up to him every morning and sharing our spare time together either staying home or going out into town, we would sometimes take Mel and Martha out for an impromptu dinner if the weather was fine. If I knew Tom was working alone in his studio I would occasionally creep up there and prepare some lunch and then curl up on the sofa with Picasso, read my book and surreptitiously watch Tom work. I still got that little flip in my stomach when we acknowledged each other with just a look. In such a short space of time he had become part of my fabric, even his little idiosyncrasies (he had a few, don't we all) did not diminish my feelings for him. I guess this was the crux of the matter. I couldn't be sure he felt the same and I just didn't know what to do with my uncertainty.

One of the many benefits of our current living arrangements was that I got to know Ailish a lot better, she would sometimes come down to eat with us in the evening or join us in the pub. I liked her a lot, a strong independent young woman who knew what she wanted in life. I recognised bits of Tom in her character, the cheeky humour, but also the gentleness in her manner with others, so I could only assume that her father Liam was a similar person .

We had gone out for a drink one evening and while Tom was at the bar I was asking Ailish about her University Course in Dublin where she was studying Art and fashion design. 'So, will you aim for modelling?'

Nearly choking on her Guinness she let out one of her famous raucous laughs.

'Feck no! I want to design clothes not wear them. I've seen how those girlies get treated sometimes and there is no way I'm

139

cutting out my grub and ale to be paraded on a cat walk! That's why my designs will be for the curvier lady, real women like!'

'Thank god, I'll drink to that!'

'Jaisus, what are you two Cailleach plotting—Ailish I could hear you cackling across to the bar!'

'Tommy boy—you can call me a witch as much as you like but don't go tarring Cassie with that brush. Sure there's not a bad bone in her body!'

Back at Sanctuary house Tom went up to the studio with Ailish to cover some of the canvases he had been working on or 'To tuck the wains in' he would say, as Ailish rolled her eyes.

I wrapped a shawl around me and stepped onto the balcony to stargaze, I didn't hear Tom come in but I felt his arms wrap around me.

'Hey you, how are the wains?'

'All good and settled for the night; Ailish was asking when I was going to take you to meet the rest of the family.'

'Ah, and what did you say?'

'I said I would see how you felt about it.'

I turned to face him, and I felt that thing that was bugging me again, I saw no indication that he was enamoured by Ailish's idea. I pulled away and walked into the sitting room.

'Ok, well I'm sensing that maybe it's you that needs time to think on it. Would I be right?'

'Well, half right--they're a tough crowd the Moynihans, and I'm not sure you're ready for them yet.'

'Well thanks for that vote of confidence Tom,' I hoped my disappointment wasn't too obvious, 'what happened to me taking a leap of faith?'

I was trembling but I wasn't sure if it was because I'd been stood outside too long or if I knew I was about to say something I would regret. I went to the cupboard and reached in for the bottle of brandy and I automatically took down two glasses. I poured one for myself but left the bottle open for Tom to help himself. I could feel him watching my every move.

'So come on then, what makes you so sure that I'm not good enough for your family?'

140

'Cass, please don't, that's not what I meant at all—in fact I'm pretty sure they'd think the world of you—I mean jaisus Ailish already says you're not a witch.'

A very brief moment of warmth for his humour or maybe from the brandy but I suddenly thought of Lucy,

'Or perhaps there's something you're keeping from me, is that it Tom?'

He looked stunned; as if I'd slapped him, he put the bottle of brandy and unused glass back in the cupboard.

'I'm dog tired Cassie, I'm away to bed now are you coming?'

'No, I think I'll just stay a while.'

It was quite some time later, when I realised I had been glued to the spot staring into space, I got up to use the bathroom. My bedroom door was open but the bed was empty and Tom had taken himself to the spare room, he was lying fully clothed on top of the unmade bed. It made me unbearably sad, so I crept to my room, curled up on my bed and wondered if I would ever be able to trust the people I love.

I was up early and already making coffee when I heard Tom in the shower, I opened the balcony doors even though it was a dull damp day; I needed the salt air hit as much as I needed the caffeine in the morning.

When Tom appeared he looked so tired and serious, I wanted to cry all over again.

'I made coffee.'

'Thanks'

'It's a mizzly day'

'Mizzly?'

'Yes, a mixture of drizzle and mist.'

'Is that a proper word?'

'It is, I think it's Cornish.'

'Or Cassish maybe?' a hint of a smile and a slow shake of the head.

'Tom—'

'Cassie, I need to talk but I need you to listen.'

'Serious stuff then.'

'Yes and no.'

'Why do you always talk in riddles?'

He threw me a look of despair.

'Sorry, go on.'

'I've lied to you'

'Oh great, well I…'

'Jaisus, Mary mother of God Cassie, can you please just let me finish?'

I clamped my mouth shut and Tom inhaled deeply.

'You remember, I told you I was scared of nothing?'

I nodded silently.

'Well it turns out; I lied to you and to myself. I *am* scared. I have never in all my years met anyone like you… Not a one Cass. I'm scared I'll blink and you'll be gone; I love you, and that's the truth right there.'

I'm not sure there is a word for the strange strangulated sound that came from my throat, part laugh, part choke, part snort but I threw myself at him and showered him with kisses.

'I'm thinking you don't mind then?' he laughed

'Eejit.'

Tom's phone was buzzing on the bedside table and once we unwrapped ourselves, he checked the message.

'Ah, it's Ailish wanting to know if I'm going into the gallery today.'

'Will you tell her?'

'What, that I'm enjoying intimate time with a mad woman?'

'Ha no, that I'll come and meet the Moynihans.'

'I'm thinking it wasn't you she was fretting about—she told me to man up and grow a pair.'

'Way to go Ailish!'

'Well, she is my big brothers wain, so in his absence she has orders to kick my arse.'

I make a mental note to thank her personally.

[30]

Ailish was due to return home to Ireland the last weekend of August, so she was delighted to hear that Tom would be closing the gallery for the Bank Holiday weekend and that we would be flying out with her on the Friday.

'Closing up shop on a holiday weekend? Tom must be serious Cass.'

I blushed to my roots.

'I think it's more a case of fitting in a visit before we both get busy in September.'

'Right, well whatever the reason, the folks at home are buzzin' to meet you!'

We flew out of Gatwick on the Friday at 4 pm and arrived in Cork Airport at 5.25 pm, so not enough time for me to get too nervous, especially with Ailish chatting ten to the dozen. We were met at the airport by Liam, an older and broader version of Tom, once he had greeted his daughter and brother he turned to me and rested his hands on my shoulders, 'Sure, here's the lovely Cassie who has stolen the boyos heart,' he held me at arms length and I imagined that this was how he appraised one of their prize cattle, but he suddenly pulled me into a big hug, 'Welcome to County Cork! Now we best get on our way, Ma's cooking up a storm and the house is heavin' right now.'

'Liam you great lummox will you stop scaring her?' Tom had slipped a reassuring hand around my waist, much gentler; the difference between a farmer and an artist's touch I guessed.

Clonakilty was roughly 25 miles from the airport and on the drive in Tom pointed out landmarks of the pretty town with its brightly painted cottages and shop fronts; I was picturing Tom as a boy running through the streets with his friends. Taking my hand he turned to me, 'Are you ok love?'

I nodded but I hadn't realised how emotional I was feeling and I struggled not to cry.

'It's beautiful Tom.'

The town gave way to undulating; lush green countryside and I even caught a glimpse of Clonakilty Bay. I already knew I

143

would want to come back and spend more time exploring this little jewel of nature. We drove up a wide farm track and I spotted the cattle in the fields beyond but I wasn't prepared for the sight of the solid white farmhouse at the end of the track, it was much bigger than I had imagined and being of a Georgian style it resembled the pictures I would draw as a child, with big square windows, a slate roof with a chimney and a sturdy red door at its centre. Outside that door there appeared to be a child excitedly hopping from one foot to another and on spotting us he turned to run inside the house.

'That's Jimmy, Caitlin's boy, gone to alert the welcoming party!' Liam laughed.

I looked to Tom, 'Ok, now I'm just a tad scared.'

He kissed my forehead just as a parade of people emerged from the house. I had visions of a never ending human snake wrapping itself around the rooms conga style. I now understood why Tom had worried about the 'full on' experience but he assured me it wouldn't be like this every time.

'Sure, I'm lucky if just me Ma comes out when I visit! Come on love, come and meet the folks.'

I was introduced to Tom's mother and father first; Maeve and Tom senior, those were two names I should be able to remember without too much trouble. I started itching for my notebook and pen when I shook hands first with the sisters, Clodagh, Bridget, Caitlin and Aisling; followed by the brothers Declan and Connor. Of course I already knew Liam but if I was expected to remember all their partners and children I didn't stand a chance. Maeve obviously picked up on this, 'Tom, let's take Cassie through for a cuppa so she can settle. Now you mustn't worry yourself pet about remembering everyone, my own wains have to correct me from time to time!'

Later, we sat down at what seemed to be a large banqueting table laden with food of every description to feed the masses. I think I lost count at 22 but there may have been more, someone told me that it wasn't unusual for everyone to gather on a holiday weekend.

There was a lot of banter and chat that carried on late into the evening but gradually everyone helped to clear the table and eventually the family dispersed into the night leaving the few who were sleeping at the house.

I found it touching that Tom and I had been given rooms next too each other, as if it was considered appropriate to be separated but leaving the option for us to sneak some time together.

When Tom crept into my room I couldn't help but stifle a giggle at the thought of two adults in their forties sneaking a goodnight kiss.

'Ah, well they put up pretence of old fashioned values, but with a family our size nothing shocks them now.'

'Well, all I know is that after initially feeling like I had walked directly into the eye of a tornado, I have never been made to feel more welcome anywhere. You are so lucky Tom, having family I mean.'

'Well, they are on their best behaviour, don't go thinking they are always this nice.'

'Hush, don't spoil it now.'

That was the last I remembered of the conversation, as within moments, I had drifted into an exhausted slumber.

The next morning I left Tom sleeping while I showered and tried to remember the way down to the kitchen. Maeve and Tom senior were sat at the kitchen table.

'Good morning Cassie love, did you sleep ok? Come sit, will you have a cuppa? Thomas has just finished his first breakfast but I can make you a bite if you'd like?'

'I slept really well and just a cup of tea would be perfect thanks Maeve. I'm guessing you have really early starts?'

'Up at 4.00am, first milking at 5.00 and in here for first breakfast around 6.30.' Tom senior smiled.

'Blimey, no wonder you need more than one breakfast!'

I was desperately trying to calculate their ages and although I was sure they must be in their seventies, I couldn't quite believe it and made a mental note to ask Tom later.

'So young Toms not up yet then?'

I was quick with my response, 'Oh, I'm not sure, I didn't hear anything this morning.'

They both glanced at each other and winked, I blushed but it confirmed what Tom had said the night before.

145

From the conversation that followed, I learnt that Liam was the only son who worked the farm with Thomas now but they did have extra labour to help too.

'Talking of Liam, its time I was out helping with the feed.'

Thomas got up from his chair and Maeve reached up to kiss his stubbly cheek.

'See you for second breakfast.'

After the door had closed behind him I poured more tea for us both.

'Goodness, this is a hard life Maeve'

'Not really love, not when it's all you've ever known. Sure sometimes are harder than others but we always make time for craic, especially at weekends like.'

I nodded, 'Thanks so much for letting me join you all this weekend.'

'Ah Cassie, you will always be welcome here,' she looked to the door and lowered her voice, 'truth is pet, we have never seen our Tom so settled, your obviously good for the lad.'

'Maeve, that's a lovely thing to say but I can assure you it works both ways.'

I didn't feel the need to elaborate and as she passed behind my chair she gently patted my back, 'Right now, I'm going to make a start on second breakfast before the rest of the house wakes up'

I insisted on helping where I could, especially when it came to setting the table in the dining room and taking food through.

'Are you some kind of food magician?' I asked as I tasted a piece of fresh baked fadge, a melt in the mouth potato bread.

'I have me ma to thank for handing down her recipes but I thank the lord for freezers!'

I soon discovered what Maeve had meant by the weekend craic. People started appearing that I had absolutely no recollection of meeting the night before; they were all ushered into the dining room whilst we finished up in the kitchen. I was just cleaning down a work surface when Tom appeared at the doorway with a huge grin on his face.

'I can't leave you alone for long can I?'

'What?'

'I've been instructed by me Ma to come and fetch 'my angel' in for breakfast!'

Once breakfast was cleared, Tom took me outside to show me around the kitchen garden where the family grew all their basic vegetables and herbs, including the all hallowed potato.

'Tom, how on earth do they do all this? I've been trying to figure out how old they are, I mean their energy and appearance gives no indication.'

'Short of searching the records, I'm not sure we know exactly, I mean Ma has been 70 for the past few years! Da is like his father before him and doesn't believe in numbers when it comes to birthdays, he just celebrates life.'

I thought of my own parents and how they had seemed forever old as oppose to the Moynihans forever young.

As if on cue Maeve appeared, 'Tom, come on darlin', you and Cass are in with Liam, can you grab one of the baskets love?'

Tom grabbed my hand dramatically.

'Awh Jais, not the basket!'

'What basket?'

'Ma's made a picnic!'

So, in Liam's Land Rover we headed the Moynihan autocade down to Inchydoney beach and judging by the acknowledging waves and nods we were getting, it wasn't an unusual occurrence. The moment we parked up, I recognised the landscape captured in some of Toms paintings; wild and exposed but with a huge expanse of golden sand just waiting to be transferred to canvas or explored by bare feet.

The kids of the Moynihan tribe were already running towards the surf, I glanced sideways at Tom and kicked off my sandals, 'Now this is what I call a beach!'

I'm not sure where the unfettered freedom came from but I was off like a greyhound from the traps...well ok, maybe more like a St Bernard down a mountain side but I was surrounded by children I didn't know, giggling, kicking and splashing.

I heard Tom laughing and shouting, 'You're a feckin crazy woman!'

When he finally caught up with me he grabbed my hand.

'Come here and walk with me.'

147

We walked and talked and I told Tom I was slightly overwhelmed by the gamut of emotions I was experiencing.

'You can't say I didn't warn you Cass'

'No that's true, but I wasn't prepared to feel a touch of sadness when I realised what both Ben and myself have missed out on.'

'Well I guess we need to make up for lost time then.'

Mid glorious snog we were interrupted by young Jimmy, acting out an over exaggerated cough, 'Morai Maeve says when youse have finished with yer appy tizers will yer be coming over for yer sangwiches?'

He turned and ran back to where everyone was sitting.

'Tom, I'm not sure I can…'

'Away with you Cass, of course you can, sure they're only joshing'

'No, I mean I don't think I can fit any more food in!'

Sitting on the picnic blanket, having somehow managed to consume a coffee and half a cheese sandwich I was thinking how much pleasure it seemed to give people to feed me up. I mean I wasn't exactly wasting away; I would have some work to do when I got back to Brighton.

'Oh god, sorry I nearly forgot,' I pulled a tin wrapped in red ribbon from my rucksack; 'Mel and Martha sent you some home made lemon cookies along with their love of course!'

We talked about M&M with great affection and it was clear that Maeve and Thomas had a soft spot for them.

'Now, there's a remarkable couple.' Thomas was shaking his head.

'Yes, you must send our love, I might just write a little card, if you don't mind passing it on like? They know they're always welcome here but we know it's not easy so maybe we will come see them soon.'

'You should ma, they'd love that but don't leave it too long ok?'

I noted the concern in Tom's voice and I knew he was thinking of the progression of Martha's illness.

The autocade headed back in time for late afternoon milking. Tom went to lend a hand whilst Maeve and I emptied the picnic baskets and washed the dishes. The rest of the family left for their own homes with promises of seeing us later.

'Please tell me you're not entertaining us all again later'

'Lord no! I get the night off on a Saturday but we're all off to the pub later for a bit of music'

'Maeve, you should bottle whatever it is you're on, you'd make a fortune!'

A night out in Clonakilty can only be described as a heart warming experience.

The bar we went to was cosy and intimate and full of traditional music, even those who weren't musicians, were joining in but only if it wasn't going to ruin the performance and otherwise there was a silence that showed great respect for their talent. As for the Guinness, I'm not sure I had tasted anything like it anywhere else and I just hoped it wouldn't spoil my taste for it back in Brighton. The evening was an ideal way to spend time with the whole family and for me to try without much success to remember everybody's name; in the end I took photos of them all and tagged them, much to their amusement.

'I hope you haven't been messing with me and swapping you're names around'

'Actually Cass, I'm really Clodagh!' Liam shouted raising his voice an octave.

Walking home, Tom was still laughing about his brother.

'Great lumox.'

I could see now what Maeve meant, he really did seem happy in his own skin.

Tom and I were booked on our return flight to Gatwick for Sunday evening, so we spent some quality time with his parents during the day and I even got a tour of the farm from Thomas senior which Tom reckoned was the biggest compliment I could wish for.

'I'll teach you to milk next time.' Thomas said with a rye smile.

'Careful now da, that's like a red rag to the bull!'

I didn't mind that they were making fun of me; it was just great to see them totally at ease with each other.

Various family popped in and out at intervals to say goodbye and we made it clear to Maeve that we would not be needing a fully cooked meal before heading off.'

'I think you should have a day off Maeve, I mean there's enough in that fridge to feed an army for the next week.'

I hoped I hadn't overstepped the mark but even Thomas senior agreed,

'Cass has a fair point love. Cold cuts never harmed a man.'

When it came to saying farewell to Thomas and Maeve, I was feeling quite choked.

'I have had such an amazing time, thank you both for making my first visit to Clon so special. You must come and see us soon, I mean we have plenty of room between the two of us and I know Mel and Martha would love to see you again.'

'We'll definitely do that soon love.'

With a pat on the cheek for me and a hug for Tom from Maeve, we climbed into Liam's car and waved till they were little specs in the distance.

When we left Gatwick for the train back to Brighton I felt in a stupefied daze,

'Did we really only leave on Friday?'

'Ah, as I've said, it'll be easier next time love. That is if you want there to be a next time?'

'You are kidding me right?'

The train from Gatwick to Brighton is quick and easy but it still felt a bit too late to knock on M&M's door, and once inside my flat we sat on the balcony with a hot drink.

'Its Bank Holiday tomorrow Cass.'

'I am aware of this fact Thomas junior.'

'So, will we be treating it as such?'

'Please don't mention food or picnics at this time of night.'

'Ha, no I was thinking more of private time like, I'm not sure I like sharing you for too long.'

'I missed you too.'

It felt so good to climb into our bed, with only the sound of our own breath for company.

[31]

The Bank Holiday started with an eerie sea fret rolling over the coast line bringing with it a blanket of silence apart from the occasional wistful cry of the gulls.

We were in no rush to go anywhere, so we enjoyed a late, lazy breakfast. I had forgotten to cancel the weekend papers so when we had arrived home on Sunday evening they were neatly piled at the bottom of the stairs. Now as we sipped our coffee, we sat opposite ends of the sofa, the floor surrounding us strewn with separated sections of broadsheets. Peaceful and relaxed in each others company we exchanged comments and quotes, swapping sections of interest. This scene of domestic bliss was interrupted by a familiar scratching at the door accompanied by a soulful mewing. Tom smiled at me;

'Uh oh, now we're in for it. Prince Picasso will want to know exactly what we were thinking, the two of us leaving him the whole weekend like!'

'Awh bless his furry paws' I said, attempting to extract myself from cosy cushions and newsprint.

'You stay right there darlin', I'll take the blame for this one.'

Tom edged his way over the room in fake trepidation and very slowly began to unlock the door.

'Come on Tom stop teasing the poor little beggar and let him in!'

The moment the door was open wide enough, Picasso shot passed him and straight onto my lap where he began purring loudly and nuzzling into my neck.

'Would you look at that now, straight in to steal my girl; sure is that all the thanks I get lad?' Tom was affectionately ruffling the cat's fur which increased the volume of Picassos purring.

'Mind he's not looking as dapper as usual, he's probably been too grumpy for Martha to give him his beauty treatment.'

'We must pop down and visit M&M this morning.'

By the time we had cleared the decks and washed the dark, smudgy news from our hands, there wasn't much left of the morning but the fret was burning off outside, which usually meant a brighter afternoon. I wondered if perhaps Mel and Martha might like a stroll along the prom, but the moment Melvin opened the door, I knew that would be out of the question. He appeared tired and drawn despite his attempt to be his usual self.

'Well now, look who rolled in with the sea fret!'

'Mel lad, how's it going?'

'It's been a bit of a tough weekend to be honest Tom, especially for the lady of the house but she's resting on the sofa now, so come on in.'

Once in the sitting room, I had to hide my shock and swallow hard to stop the tightness in my throat. The usually bright room was closed to the outside world and apart from the gentle lamps there was barely any light at all. Lying on the sofa, propped up by layers of cushions and pillows was a Martha I hardly recognised, her snowy white hair fell loosely around her shoulders and her waxen pallor meant that she almost blended into the white linen surrounding her.

Tom moved swiftly passed me to her side and took her hand,

'Martha darlin', I can't leave you two alone for a moment can I now? Why didn't youse call me you know we would've come.'

'Now then Tom, you know I never want to be a party pooper,' even her voice sounded crumpled and her breathing was shallow, 'besides... I want to hear all about your weekend; Cassie darling girl....was it wonderful?'

I stepped forward and leaned in to kiss her cold cheek,

'It was more than wonderful Martha, and I promise we will tell you every detail...but right now I can hear your Mel crashing about in the kitchen, so I'm going to rescue him, ok?'

She nodded with a weak smile, I touched Tom's shoulder as I moved away and he reached up to squeeze my hand.

In the kitchen, beams of weak light were working their way over the worktops and through the window I could see parts of the garden emerging from the salt laden mist. Mel was leaning against the sink, staring out as if he was searching for an explanation.

'Mel, let me help.'

152

At the sound of my voice, his hands covered his face and his chin dropped to his chest as a restrained sob left his lips. Wrapping my arms around him, I held him till his weeping subsided then I guided him to the kitchen table and gently sat him down.

Tom appeared in the doorway,

'Martha's sleeping, are you up to chatting Mel?'

I busied myself making the pot of tea that Mel had started on, while he explained the events of the last few days.

'Martha had been just fine for a while now, but on Friday, not so long after you had left, she said she felt awful tired. I suggested she go for a proper lie down on the bed. You know how stubborn she can be; but eventually she agreed to go rest, as long as I promised to wake her after an hour.'

I took a seat with them at the table and poured the tea.

'Thank you bubele,' Mel wrapped his hands around the cup, 'so, after an hour I went to look in on her; and I knew then she was struggling,' his voice caught and he cleared his throat, 'I haven't seen her with such a rigor for a very long time. So I called the surgery.'

Mel told us that the gp had responded immediately and an ambulance was with them in what seemed a matter of minutes, followed closely by the doctor himself who was very familiar with Martha's medical history. They took her to hospital where she was given a barrage of tests and she was monitored whilst they reviewed her condition and medication.

'I stayed with meyn lib all through the night and Saturday too...but by Sunday she was fussing to come home,' he smiled, 'she wanted to be here when you got back...what is it you kids call it? Fomo?'

Tom and I didn't know whether to laugh or cry. Mel told us that the Macmillan nurse and the doctor were due to come by on Tuesday morning when hopefully they would be able to discuss the test results, but until then, complete rest was the order of the day.

'Well, I'm thinking that applies to the two of you, so how about I stay here tonight? Just to make sure you do as you're told like.'

There was an instant look of relief on Mel's face,

'Tom, that would be a great kindness, it would mean I could catch up on some rest, I need to stay strong for my Martha.'

So it was agreed that we would go and organise a few things and that Tom would return for the night. Back in my flat, we stood on the balcony holding each other so tightly that I wondered if we could ever be separated again; in the midst of all the sadness I realised that my love for Tom was growing deeper and stronger the more I got to know him.

'I won't come back down with you love, but I will keep my phone by me, please call me at any time through the night if you need me.'

With one last kiss, he left to be with Martha and Mel.

[32]

Apart from a late night text telling me all was well, I hadn't heard from Tom and hoped that this was a good sign. I had dreamt of my mother during the night and when I woke, my face was damp with tears and my heart heavy with guilt. I couldn't help thinking that I hadn't spent as much time with her as I should have and that possibly she had died not knowing just how much I loved her and that I would do my utmost to take care of my father. Of course, at 18 years old I had struggled to make any sense of my emotions and had been left feeling inadequate and angry.

Early Tuesday morning I rang Tom to ask if I should bring some breakfast down.

'Hey darlin', the doctor and nurse have just arrived but Martha and Mel wondered if you could come and join us.'

'I'm on my way.'

There was an unexpected change in the atmosphere as I walked through to the sitting room and compared to the previous day, everything was a little brighter. The curtains were open which gave a lighter aspect to the whole room. The nurse was putting the finishing touches to Martha's hair which gave her an almost regal appearance, as if she were about to hold court with her loyal subjects; when she spotted me her beautiful eyes sparkled but there was no denying that she was still struggling.

'Here's my girl' she lifted her hand and I was quickly by her side.

The information we received over the following hour was painful to hear but it was clearly evident that M&M had been expecting it and they had possibly been preparing for this moment for quite some time.

Follicular lymphoma is a cruel illness that gives false hope time and again by allowing the body to go into remission in response to medication, only to return and attack any vulnerability it can get its' evil clutches on.

Martha's low grade illness had advanced to a high grade stage 3; basically her lymphomas were spreading. Medications would no longer give her remissions but they may give her a little more time.

Palliative care would commence and Martha and Mel had chosen the option of hospice care for three days a week to begin with, and home care for the remaining four days.

Once all the details had been finalised and the nurse had made Martha comfortable, we were left alone with M&M. Martha insisted on hearing about our Irish trip and we even managed to raise some smiles with stories of my first meeting with the Moynihans. Aware of how tired they both were, we thought it best to leave them to spend some much needed time together. Tom suggested we go for a walk and we headed to the boardwalk, 'How are you doing love?' I asked.

'Not sure it's hit me yet. Martha in particular has always been honest and open with me like, so after all the discussions we've had over the years, I didn't think this would be such a shock... but it feels like a kick in the guts you know?'

'Life is so fucking unfair.'

'Ah not always.'

I looked at him aghast.

'How can you even say that?'

'Oh,what? So you think it's unfair for two people to meet against all the odds, spend the whole of their lives loving each other; sharing a dream to give others a slice of their happiness? Jaisus Cass, I wouldn't call that unfair, I'm thinking they'd count themselves lucky.'

'No, no, I don't think any of that stuffs unfair....'

'What then?'

'It's when all of that is shattered and someone is left to pick up the pieces.'

Life at Sanctuary house would never be the same again, but of course I knew that and I remembered at the beginning of our relationship, Tom warning me, 'Nothing in the world stands still'

Martha had been having palliative home care for a couple of weeks; I had started my job at the university and Tom had made the trip to Ireland to set up his exhibition and give his talk to the students. I would call in on M&M every day after work staying as long or as little as the situation dictated. Each time I placed my key in their door, I would close my eyes and visualize Martha as she was when I first arrived at the house but of course that Martha never materialised and I would often climb the stairs to my flat with a feeling of such sadness that each step was like wearing shackles.

Tom and I kept Andy and Ray in the loop as their visits were kept to a minimum, mainly to avoid tiring Martha but also too much contact from outside was discouraged. I could tell this was not what she wanted, but she was too weak to argue.

Mel barely left her side and consequently he took on the appearance of a waning sentinel. No music, no laughter, no hope.

I can't deny that I had welcomed starting work, although it carried a familiar sense of guilt, as if I was trying to escape, but my Sanctuary house had become anything but the safe haven I was accustomed to.

During my first week I really wanted to make a good impression but I felt it was only fair to explain my home situation; unsurprisingly Imani was kind and supportive telling me to let her know if I was struggling.

Ben still called me once a week which always left me feeling calmer and more focused, he intended to come and stay with us during reading week at the beginning of November.

'Are you sure love? I mean, sadly it isn't a great time right now.'

'Ma, I want to be there, ok?'

Lucy had already decamped to France and although we had to cancel her weekend stay, we still managed to spend a day in Lewes before she left. We talked about maybe Tom and me taking a trip to France in the New Year.

'The New Year Cass! That will be almost a year since you began your journey.'

'God, I know Luce! But you do know that journeys never officially end?'

'Hippy'

'Always'

157

I cried all the way home.

The second week of October was truly autumnal. The sky was a magnificent cerulean blue, scattered with wings of feathery clouds; the sea appeared to join this gentle homage to nature, sparkling and singing its way across the shingle.

I cycled to work. It seemed a long time since I had felt the briny breeze against my skin and I arrived feeling calm and relaxed.

The previous day, Mel, Tom and I had met with the doctor and nurse at Martha's bedside. They told us that there was a permanent room waiting at the hospice for her whenever she felt the time was right. Initially and understandably, Mel struggled with the idea until Martha whispered wearily, 'Mel, honey, a bed's a bed, and you will still be sitting right by me wherever that may be. I think its time I had a change of scene.'

'Of course meyn lib' he said kissing her hand tenderly.

Mel and Martha had granted Tom power of attorney a long time ago knowing how difficult Mel would find official paperwork, but Tom always spent time explaining every detail to both of them before any signatures were given. He had stayed downstairs long after I had left to complete all the necessary paperwork. When he finally crept into our bed, I wrapped myself around him waiting for his body to relax fully before falling asleep.

I got on very well with all my colleagues at the University, but I enjoyed working alongside Imani most of all. I felt I learnt such a lot from her and she was very patient with me. We had just completed a discussion with a student who had concerns over the course he had chosen; under Imani's guidance we had talked him through the many options he had and he seemed a lot happier when he left the room.

'I think we deserve a coffee' she smiled.

My phone began to buzz.

'Lovely, but is it ok if I get this?'

'Of course, no problem'

It was Tom.

'Hey you…'

158

'Cass darlin'..' His voice sounded strained and I knew immediately.

'Can you make it home love? She's asking after you.'

I remember Imanis arm around me and as she sat me down on the nearest chair, she took my phone.

'Hello Tom? This is Imani, Cassies colleague. I will drive her home.'

It was all a bit of a blur but once in Imani's car, someone handed me my coat and bag.

'Cassie, do you need a moment or shall I get you straight home?'

'Straight home please, she's asking for me. Imani, thank you so much, I'm so sorry.'

'Listen, I am going to drop you right outside the door but please let me know if you need any help over the coming days.'

Dropping everything in the hallway, I ran through the flat till I reached Martha; taking her hands in mine I thought how cold she felt and I was saddened that I couldn't bring her warmth. I could barely hear her tissue thin voice and though her beautiful eyes searched my face, they were lost to a milky glaze and their usual vibrant blue was fading slowly as she whispered,

'Darling girl...don't cry...look at how I'm dancing-- Do you know, that with true love, anything is possible?'

I kissed her forehead and struggled to speak,

'My Martha, you have taught *me* to dance again...I'll always love you for that.'

No longer able to control my grief I left the room and sat at the bottom of the stairs sobbing till Tom came out to join me, he took me in his arms and I could feel his heart slowly breaking. Martha was gone.

The following weeks were taken up with making arrangements for Martha's funeral and contacting M&M's friends and our families. I mainly spent time with Mel, the doctor had prescribed medication which helped him sleep. Tom and I both stayed with him at night and during the day we took turns in gently coaxing him to eat and also to explain the arrangements that were being made.

Martha's instructions for her funeral were simple but detailed and Tom was touched that she had tried to make the process easier for everyone.

'God love her. I think her main concern was that we watched over Mel.'

Ben came back earlier than planned so that he was in time for the funeral, Lucy also travelled from France and Tom's parents joined us as soon as they heard the news. Sanctuary house became like a hotel with people staying in every available room; even Ray and Andy offered up their spare bedroom.

The wake was held at a sea front hotel and when I look back now, I realise how surreal it all was. So many people from Martha's rich life who obviously needed to be there, but who I couldn't connect with, I had been a part of that life for less than a year, what right did I have to be there?

It was such a relief to leave them all behind and head back to the house for our own private wake, just us. Immediate family and house mates gathered around a fire pit, with just the cover of a gazebo, wrapped in scarves and blankets drinking and remembering our dear, darling Martha. The fairy lights and candles glittered and danced just as she had done through out her glorious life. I spotted Mel heading into the house and was about to follow, but Tom lay a hand on my arm,

'Let him alone love, I think I know where he's going.'

Moments later the gentle notes of Rhapsody in Blue were drifting through to the garden.

The next day I contacted Imani and asked if I could take some holiday while we tried to get some normality back to the house once all our guests had left.

'You will do no such thing! I think we can manage for a few more weeks, just let me know when you feel ready. You will need your holidays for happier times'

Ben stayed on through reading week, but I'm pretty sure not much reading was achieved. Once everyone had left, I wanted the house to inspire me as it had in the past but instead it just felt like an empty shell.

[33]

I sensed that with Martha's passing, we had all lost our way.

We moved back into my flat together but Tom continued to work in his studio, sometimes staying long into the night, sometimes not returning to me at all, He re-opened the gallery so that I barely saw him during the day either. The support team at Macmillan's continued to care for Mel, but each time I visited him, he showed no interest in small talk and seemed to stare past me as though searching for something that was not there.

Of course, I recognised all the signs of grief in both Mel and Tom but I was at a loss as to where I could fit into the equation. I decided the best thing was for me to return to work at the University in the last week of November.

Then one day, I was sat alone on my balcony, shivering with cold, I had no idea where Tom was; I just felt so defeated and alone that I began to wonder, if I left the house right now, would it really matter? A huge pear drop tear escaped down my face, soon to be followed by a torrent that would not stop. My phone buzzed and I was surprised to see a message from Tom; surprised because it was a rare event these days and also because even now, he still managed to fill my soul with longing.

'HEY CASS, WOULD YOU FANCY A PUB LUNCH?'

'HEY YOU, WHAT'S THE OCCASION?'

'NO OCCASION. JUST THINK WE SHOULD TALK.'

I know people say you shouldn't judge a text by its tone, but I couldn't ignore that sinking feeling in the pit of my stomach.

'I WAS GOING TO LOOK IN ON MEL.'

'MEL HAS VISITORS, WOULD YOU JUST COME DOWN TO THE GALLERY, PLEASE?'

I already looked a mess, and with the threat of more tears before I even left the flat, I didn't see the point of 'looking my best'.

I resisted the temptation to see who Mel's visitors were and went straight to the gallery. Tom had already locked up and he was stood on the boardwalk looking out onto a grey, choppy sea, his face unusually pale and tight lipped. I felt my heart miss a beat.

'Tom, what is it?'

Taking in my appearance, his face softened.

'We need to talk darlin'.'

A slither of comfort that he was still using my favourite term of endearment.

'And you thought out here in the cold was a good place to do that?'

'I thought we could grab a bite like'

'I'm not hungry Tom, but I'll walk with you.'

We started to walk up and passed the house when he suddenly stopped.

'Cass, I can't do this anymore.'

'Well guess what Tom? I can't do this anymore either. Not that you would know that, because you won't tell me what's going on and I'm not a mind reader. In case you've forgotten, I'm no stranger to being dumped but I am quite partial to a bit of honesty!'

I glared at him and turned on my heel. In my flat I was pacing up and down, still with the bloody sobbing. You know in the movies when the leading lady is heart broken, yet still has impeccable make up and just one strategically placed tear rolling down her cheek? Well that's bollocks.

Tom came through the door and he didn't look great either.

'Cassie love, lets sit – we need to talk.'

So, he made tea and talked while I listened.

There were two revelations to impart to me. Firstly Mel and Martha had agreed that Mel would not stay on at Sanctuary house after her death. They had in fact secured a small flat within an assisted housing complex close to the Hospice, so that when the time came, he could be close by; but of course, as it happened Martha didn't get to make it that far, but the property was all ready for Mel and he had no desire to stay on in the house without her. Secondly, Andy and Ray felt that with their imminent wedding they would like to upsize and buy a house to mark a fresh start to their new life together.

Tom had put in an offer on their flat which they had accepted.

I wasn't sure how much turmoil a body could take, so I sat for a moment in stunned silence.

'I can't be here any more Cassie.'

'Where will you go?'

'I've not decided yet. Maybe Cornwall.'

I shook my head in disbelief.

'So, you'll sell Sanctuary?'

He nodded.

'And the gallery?'

'Probably let that go too.'

'How much notice do I get?'

'Sorry?'

'You know, notice to leave YOUR property, I mean you can't sell with a squatter in residence.'

'I thought maybe you might come with me like.'

'Oh, so it didn't cross your mind to talk to me about all this when you found out?'

'Yes, it did but it never seemed a good time.'

'Oh and this is a good time? I think maybe its best that you leave me alone for a while now Tom.' I turned my back to him and without any argument he left the flat.

I didn't leave my flat for two days, living on coffee and dry toast, torturing myself with music by Green Day and other memory evoking bands. It was a purely self indulgent process; a throw back from the past; but I was sure this particular flaw in my character wasn't unique and besides I could never sustain it for too long.

In the shower I was trying hard to sing 'pick yourself up, dust yourself off and start all over again' but I really don't sing well at the best of times. I was just thinking that Picasso would give a far better rendition of my current performance, when Martha crept into my thoughts.

'Dear girl, with true love anything is possible.'

I missed having her to talk to and her motherly advice. I quickly dressed and ran down to Mel.

'Hey Mel-are you decent?'

'Bubele is that you?'

In the sitting room there was evidence of the start of packing but it was the smell of coffee coming from the kitchen that drew me in.

'Just in time Cass, you look like you need feeding up…none of Martha's muffins I'm afraid but I do got bagels.'

We talked and talked, it was so good to see Mel re-emerging and looking a little like his old self. It was as though the decision to move had given him something to focus on. I remembered that feeling well. I asked him if it would be hard to leave.

'Oh I don't think so, Martha and I never planned on staying forever, but she knew I would never leave her behind!'

I must have looked puzzled.

'You know Bubele, Martha and I wanted you and Tom to be happy'

'Oh, and we were Mel—so ridiculously happy.'

'Yes and we saw that …that's when we discovered that it wasn't the building but the people in it who brought the happiness. I dreamt of meyn lib last night… oy vey, I miss her so much Cassie, but she no longer lives here in this house. My staying here won't bring her back, she lives here in my heart now' Mel put his hand to his chest. Taking both my hands in his he continued, 'Bubele. Our Tom... he loves you so very much but he is real confused right now, and as much as you're hurting, you can bet he's hurting more.'

'How can you know that he loves me Mel?'

'Because he told us of course.'

I left Mel and ran upstairs to get my phone; there was a message already waiting.

'HEY DARLIN', IF YOU'RE NOT TOO MAD AT ME, CAN I COME OVER?'

'OH, I'M STILL MAD AT YOU BUT SURE, I GUESS YOU CAN COME OVER.'

I opened the door five minutes later.

'Forgot your key?'

'Well I didn't want to assume like'

I looked up at him and sighed,

'Tom, I'm so sorry about the other day, I really wasn't thinking straight. I mean; how could I forget just how deeply you are connected to this house, to Mel and Martha.'

'No love, I'm such an eejit and I'm fecking useless when it comes to explaining stuff'

I could tell he was waiting for me to disagree.

'I agree.'

'Well now that's a bit harsh ...but anyways, I've got a plan.'

'Uh-oh'

'No really- listen now, I know how much you love it here in Brighton and what with your new job and all, you've not really had the time to enjoy all it has to offer... so I'm thinking we should stay put for now; but in a different house, something just for the two of us like?'

'I thought you were desperate to leave, what about Cornwall?'

'Sure Cornwall will always be there.'

'You mean you'd stay... for me?'

'Ah, come here to me mo cuishle.'

'Mahushla? Is that even a proper word?'

'No, actually it's two proper words. Mo cuishle—pulse of my heart.'

***

We spent Christmas at Sanctuary house. Ben came with Kate on Christmas Eve and stayed till Boxing Day before visiting Kate's parents; he didn't seem too surprised to hear about the mass exodus from the house.

'No point staying somewhere if it makes you feel sad ma, Sanctuary has served its purpose, it's the happy memories you keep with you that count.'

'Hippy'

'It's genetic!'

It was my first and last Christmas at Sanctuary house. On Boxing Day, Tom and I visited Mel at his new flat, I think he tried very hard to appear content but it must have been so very difficult for him. When Tom and I returned to the house, I commented on how strange it was to be the last two residents. The empty house felt desolate and lonely, so we raised a glass to the way it used to be and to all the happiness it had brought to so many. Tom and I recognised how lucky we were to be a part of Sanctuary's history, but we both knew it was time for new beginnings.

By the end of January the house was sold to a well known developer who was commissioned to create student accommodation. They seemed keen to preserve the aesthetics of the building and the aim was to provide affordable housing for the ever growing student population of Brighton and Hove.

The building would keep the name of Sanctuary House above the door.

It is mid-February now and almost a year since I first set my heart on Brighton. Tom and I have moved into a house on Marine Parade, we are just around the corner from Andy and Ray and within walking distance from Mel. I'm sure Martha would approve. Tom still has his gallery, which means we often walk up to Sanctuary house and from time to time we take a peek to see how work is progressing. I kid myself that I'm only interested to see how some of 'my' future students will be living in that beautiful space. It is getting easier.

I have learnt to let go of the past and enjoy all that the present has to offer. I have also learnt that being loved means accepting that you're worthy of that privilege…no more self doubt, well most of the time anyway. Nobody knows what the future holds and who knows where we will be this time next year; but a wise and beautiful lady once told me, that with true love anything is possible, and we aim to do our best to prove her right.

****

Milton Keynes UK
Ingram Content Group UK Ltd.
UKHW050835131123
432404UK00008B/8